THE BET'S ON!

"You know, I've been thinking about this bet we've got going," said Gabriel.

"Oh?" Stevie's heart began to beat faster. Maybe Gabriel was about to chicken out!

"Yeah. In fact, I've been thinking about it all day."

Stevie smiled to herself. He was trying to find a way to weasel out of it! Maybe there was a chance they could forget this whole thing. "And?" she asked hopefully.

"And I've just decided what I'm going to make you do when I win!" he announced gleefully.

"When you *win*?" she repeated as she felt her face heat up with both anger and disappointment.

"Yeah. When I win. It's really going to be great!"

"Well, before you start enjoying your little dare too much, you'd better start worrying about what I'm going to make you do when *I* win," retorted Stevie quickly. "It'll go down in the annals of rodeo history!"

THE SADDLE CLUB

QUARTER
HORSE

BONNIE BRYANT

A SKYLARK BOOK
NEW YORK • TORONTO • LONDON • SYDNEY • AUCKLAND

RL 5, 009–012

QUARTER HORSE

A Bantam Skylark Book / September 1998

ISBN 0-553-48632-2

Published simultaneously in the United States and Canada.

*I would like to express my special thanks
to Sallie Bissell for her help
in the writing of this book.*

"JUST A FEW MORE minutes and I'll be there!" Stevie whispered happily as she guided her horse through a shallow creek of gurgling blue water. It had been a perfect day—the weather had been warm, the sunlight had sparkled, and a gentle breeze had carried the smell of blooming wildflowers. Now, as the sun was beginning to set, the whole western half of the sky glowed with a rosy light.

"It's going to be so romantic," Stevie anticipated out loud. "He'll be waiting for me at Pioneer Rock. Then we'll walk our horses along the mesa trail; then, just as the sun disappears below the horizon, he'll take me in his arms and . . ." She closed her eyes with a shiver of delight, then sat forward in the saddle and urged Belle faster. "Come on, Belle, let's hurry! We don't want to be late!"

Stevie looked down at Belle. It seemed funny. She couldn't remember bringing her own horse on this trip, but it was Belle she was riding. Her mount had the same thick, dark mane, the same easy canter, and the same familiar whinny Stevie had come to love. She was definitely on board Belle, and Belle was taking her to meet Phil.

Wait. Stevie frowned as Belle cantered faster. Wasn't Phil out rafting on a river with his family? Hadn't he invited Stevie to go along? That she remembered clearly. Now, if Phil was out on some river, then who was Belle taking her to meet?

Suddenly Belle began to slow down. They were nearing Pioneer Rock, but oddly, someone had constructed an ice cream shop there. A familiar red-and-white awning shaded the tables and chairs in the front window. Stevie blinked in amazement. It was TD's, their hangout in Virginia! A tall figure was waiting for her by the front door. *There's Phil,* she thought, smiling as Belle carried her closer. *I can tell by the way he stands with his hands in his pockets.*

Stevie looked more closely at the figure by the door. *Wait. Phil's not that tall, and his hair's not that dark, and he never wears a cowboy hat.* Suddenly she pulled hard on Belle's right rein. Phil wasn't standing there waiting for her! Gabriel was!

"No!" Stevie cried, sitting up straight, her heart pounding. Droplets of cold sweat ran down her neck, and for a moment she couldn't catch her breath. Where was she? Where was Phil? And where was Belle?

She looked around and forced herself to take several deep, slow breaths. Carole and Lisa lay on either side of her, their sleeping bags pulled up to their chins. Ten covered wagons made a large circle around them, and in the middle of that circle, Stevie could see the orange glow of a banked campfire.

"Now I remember," she whispered. "We're here, out West, reenacting part of the pioneers' journey on the Oregon Trail." A week before, Deborah Hale, Max Regnery's wife, had asked The Saddle Club to join her on this trip and help her do field research for an article she was supposed to write. Deborah had had to return unexpectedly to Virginia, but Jeremy Barksdale, the wagon master, had offered to take The Saddle Club girls under his wing so that they could complete the trip. Now here they were, wearing genuine pioneer clothes, eating genuine pioneer food, driving one covered wagon, three horses, and a cow along part of the Oregon Trail.

"Whew!" Stevie wiped the sweat from the back of her neck as she remembered with a shudder how it felt to have Belle carrying her toward obnoxious Gabriel. "Thank goodness that was only a dream." She plumped up her pillow. "Or I should say nightmare."

Stevie and the other girls had met Gabriel their first day out West. Though he was just another participant in the wagon train reenactment, Jeremy had made him assistant trail boss because he knew so much history about the Oregon Trail. Gabriel was tall and handsome and rode like a dream, but Stevie thought he was the biggest jerk on the planet. Throughout the trip his know-it-all attitude had been almost unbearable. Once he'd given her a long lecture when he'd mistakenly thought she was trying to race her team of horses; then he'd tried to outdo her in ghost-story telling; then he'd informed her that the only rodeo event she was fit to enter was the cow chip tossing contest!

"Jerk," Stevie muttered as she settled back down in her sleeping bag. "Now he's even intruding in my dreams. If this keeps up, I'll be afraid to go to sleep!" She rolled over and closed her eyes. She needed to get some rest. On the wagon train their days started at five-thirty and did not end until sunset.

She took a few more deep breaths and tried to concentrate on something pleasant—like Phil. *He's so cute*, Stevie thought with a smile. *He's got such pretty green eyes and such a nice smile*. Suddenly Gabriel's face appeared before her—his deep blue eyes sparkling as he smiled, and—Stevie shook her head, evaporated Gabriel, and again pictured Phil. *He's got such a nice laugh*, she thought. *And he looks so good on his horse, Teddy*. Again Gabriel materialized. He, too, had a nice laugh, when he was laughing *with* her instead of *at* her, and he sat his quarter horse as if he'd been born on it. Stevie sighed and tried to force her thoughts back to all the wonderful times

4

she'd had with Phil when suddenly the cute little dimple in Gabriel's cheek flashed through her head.

"This just isn't working!" she said, more awake than ever. She turned over and plunged her fist into her pillow. "I'm going to try counting sheep." She closed her eyes and pictured sheep leaping over the corral fence. Their white coats were fluffy and they baaed as they leaped through the air, but she found herself wondering where they would go and what they would do, and whether they would be able to find their way back to the corral. Her eyes flew open again. She sighed once more and rolled over.

"Maybe this time I'll try horses," she whispered as she punched her pillow a second time. "I'll start with the first horse I ever knew and work my way up." She pictured the first horse she had ever climbed on—a Shetland pony named Brownie. She had been three years old, and her mother had snapped a picture of her. *Wonder what ever happened to Brownie,* Stevie thought, her mind veering off in another direction. *I wonder if he's still giving little kids rides at that carnival . . . I wonder if he still has those shaggy blond bangs.* She'd just begun to worry if they were giving an old pony like Brownie the right kind of feed when she opened her eyes and sat up in her sleeping bag once again.

"This is terrible," she whispered, looking over at Carole and Lisa as they slept peacefully under the starry sky. "If I try to think of Phil, I think of Gabriel. If I try to count sheep, I start wondering where they go when they leave the corral. And when I think of all the horses I've known, I worry about what's become of them." She looked at the ghostly shapes of the covered-wagon tops. *I wonder what the pioneers counted when they had insomnia. Probably all the aches and pains they got from riding in their wagons*, she decided, wiggling around to make her sore rear end more comfortable.

Suddenly she grinned. "I've got it," she whispered. "The perfect solution. It's endless and boring enough to put me right to sleep." She fluffed her pillow for the final time and rolled over on her side. Smiling, she closed her eyes and began counting softly to herself.

"The first annoying thing Gabriel did was stand up and brag about how only brave *men* opened up the West. . . . The second annoying thing Gabriel did was to insinuate that I didn't know how to hitch up a team of horses to a wagon. . . . The third annoying thing Gabriel did was to tell me that in the old days menfolk never relied on womenfolk. . . . The fourth annoying thing . . ." Stevie was just about to recount what the fourth annoying thing was when her eyelids fluttered once and she finally fell into a deep and dreamless sleep.

"STEVIE!" THE NEXT THING Stevie heard was a voice, calling from somewhere above her head.

"Hmmmpf," she replied, snuggling back down in her

sleeping bag and trying to reenter the dream she was having about Phil.

"Stevie, wake up! We're going to delay the whole wagon train if we don't get going!"

Stevie opened one eye. Lisa stood above her, already wearing the pioneer dress she'd worn throughout the trip. Her hair was combed back behind her ears, and her blue eyes looked rested from a good night's sleep.

"What time is it?" Stevie croaked.

"It's almost six. Everyone's already eating breakfast."

Stevie rubbed her eyes. Carole and Lisa, dressed in their pioneer clothes, were looking down at her. "You guys go on. I'll catch up to you in a few minutes."

"You won't go back to sleep, will you?" Carole asked dubiously.

"No." Stevie shook her head. "I'm awake. I'll be there as soon as I get dressed."

Stevie crawled out of her sleeping bag while Carole and Lisa walked over to the chuck wagon. On the far side of the circle she could see Shelly Bean, the camp cook, dishing out the hot cornmeal mush that everyone ate for breakfast. Quickly she rolled up her sleeping bag and climbed into the wagon. After she stashed her pillow and blankets, she pulled on her own scratchy dress and brushed her teeth in the bucket of water that Lisa had hung behind the driver's seat. Stevie gave her hair a quick brushing, then jumped out of the wagon. As she walked over to join her friends for breakfast, she noticed that an air of excitement hung over the wagon train. Today was their last full day on the trail. That afternoon they would roll into Clinchport and start preparing for the local rodeo.

"Morning, Stevie," Polly Shaver called from the back of her wagon. Polly was a dance instructor from Cleveland and one of the new friends the girls had made on their trip. She pointed her camera at Stevie, then lowered it again. "I was going to take your picture, but you look a little tired."

"I didn't sleep too well," Stevie replied with a yawn.

"You must have been dreaming about the rodeo," Polly teased.

"I wish." Stevie shook her head as she walked over to Lisa and Carole. *More like I was having nightmares about the dumb old assistant trail boss*, she thought glumly.

"Hi, Stevie. Glad you made it." Carole stepped forward as Stevie slipped into line behind her. Carole wore her long dark hair in a single braid so that her cowboy hat would fit easily on her head. "Did you have trouble sleeping last night? I vaguely remember you sitting up and mumbling something about counting sheep."

"I had a terrible night last night," grumbled Stevie as she grabbed a tin cup and plate. "Sheep were only a few of the things I tried to count."

The breakfast line inched forward. "Why, here come

8

my three favorite girls from Virginia." Shelly grinned through his curly gray beard as the girls neared his steaming pot of mush. "Step right up here and let me give you a good, hot breakfast. You'll need lots of energy if we're gonna roll into Clinchport today."

Shelly loaded their plates. Then they dipped out some milk from the bucket on the chuck wagon and sat down close to the fire. Though the sun was up, last night's chill had not left the air. The girls ate quickly and hurried back to their wagon to get ready to go. Lisa packed up their gear while Stevie and Carole went to the corral to get Yankee, Doodle, and Nikkia, their horses. The girls had just started to lead them back to the wagon when they saw Gabriel walking toward them.

"Oh, brother," Stevie sighed as she pulled Yankee and Doodle along behind her. "Here comes Mr. Know-It-All."

"Maybe he won't be such a jerk today," Carole whispered, holding Nikkia's halter as Gabriel sauntered up to them wearing his usual smug smile.

"Hi, ladies," he said, tipping his cowboy hat. "I noticed you were late for breakfast. Is your wagon going to be ready for the final push to Clinchport?"

"It is," snapped Stevie.

"Well, you'll be driving behind Mr. Cate's wagon today," he said. "It's your turn to ride drag."

"No kidding," Stevie muttered.

9

Gabriel smirked. "And you might want to consider wearing a bonnet and a bandanna over your nose. I'd hate for all that nasty dust to mess up your hair."

"Thanks for thinking of us, Mr. Assistant Trail Boss," Stevie said. "I don't know what we womenfolk would do without you."

"My pleasure," he said, striding off to help Karen Nicely with her horse's bridle.

"Ugh." Stevie clenched her fists. "Sometimes he makes me so mad I don't know what to do."

"Just take it easy, Stevie," said Carole. "We've only got one more day to put up with him as assistant trail boss."

"You're right," Stevie said as she led the two big quarter horses to the wagon traces. "How bad can it be?"

A few minutes later, The Saddle Club was ready to roll. Stevie took her usual place driving the wagon, and Carole rode Nikkia alongside. Lisa was in charge of Veronica, the milk cow, who more or less ambled along behind her. In the past five days the girls had grown accustomed to their pioneer jobs and now did them easily and well. Stevie watched for Jeremy's signal to roll forward as she gathered the reins in her hand.

"Oooh, do you have to ride in the back today?" a small voice called. Stevie peered down in front of the horses. There stood Eileen, the eight-year-old brat whose wailing over a lost teddy bear had caused a cattle stampede two nights before. It was only through Carole's quick thinking and The Saddle Club's great teamwork with Gabriel that an entire herd of rampaging longhorns had been diverted away from the wagon train encampment.

"Yes, we are," said Stevie. "And I thought you were supposed to be riding in the back of your parents' wagon."

"I was," replied Eileen. "But I apologized so hard for everything I'd done and I cried so many tears over it that they let me out." She gave Stevie a sly grin. "They said now I can go anywhere I want."

"Oh?" Stevie raised one eyebrow.

"Yes. I could even stand here in front of your wagon all day if I wanted to."

"You might get run over," Stevie pointed out.

"I would not! You wouldn't dare run over me!"

"Oh, brother," Stevie said to herself. She was just about to reply when Eileen's mother called to her daughter in an irritated voice. In a flash, the little girl had turned and was running toward her own wagon. "Saved by the bell," Stevie muttered.

Slowly the wagons began to move forward. Stevie popped Yankee and Doodle's reins and took her place at the end of the line. Farther ahead, Lisa and Veronica were posing for Polly's camera, and Carole had ridden Nikkia forward to help someone sort out a nervous horse. At the head of the wagon train, Stevie could see Gabriel, leading the way.

"Why am I dreaming about him, of all people?" she began to wonder out loud. She frowned. "I don't even like him. And if I'm dreaming about somebody I don't even like, then who in the world is Phil dreaming about?" Ever since the trip had begun, Stevie had fought a niggling worry that Phil might have met a new girl on his rafting trip—a cuter, smarter, more fun girl than she was. Even though Carole and Lisa had told her that she was being silly and that it was just not possible, she hadn't been able to shake the uneasy feeling from her mind.

She yawned, then clucked to Yankee and Doodle. "If I'm dreaming about somebody I can't stand, then Phil must be having cyberoptic, digitized visions of his dream girl," Stevie said grumpily. "He's probably so sleepy every morning, he can barely stay on his raft!"

THE WAGON TRAIN rolled into Clinchport late that afternoon, making its usual wide circle on a grassy plateau that overlooked the rodeo grounds. Stevie drove Yankee and Doodle up just behind Mr. Cate's wagon and pulled on the parking brake.

"I guess that's where the action's going to be." Mr. Cate hopped off his wagon and shielded his eyes as he gazed down at the flat plain where a wide horse-racing track adjoined a large arena. Red, white, and blue bunting hung from the grandstand and American flags fluttered festively from every available pole. He grinned over at Stevie. "Are you excited about the rodeo?"

"I sure am," Stevie replied as she began to unhitch Yankee and Doodle. "But right now I'm more excited about not having to drive that bumpy wagon anymore."

13

"They could use some shock absorbers, couldn't they?" Mr. Cate drawled in his soft Alabama accent. He rubbed his back. "Maybe the pioneers were just better padded than we are."

The wagon train made camp. Working smoothly as a team, The Saddle Club soon had their horses unhitched and their campsite ready for the night. Carole unsaddled Nikkia and helped Stevie take Yankee and Doodle to the makeshift corral, while Lisa gave Veronica some hay and brought a fresh bucket of water from the creek. They had just finished their chores when Jeremy's voice rang out from the center of the encampment.

"Congratulations, all you pioneers!" he said as everyone gathered around him. "We've made it to the end of the trail, and our worst catastrophe was the dousing of one teddy bear!" Everyone laughed except Eileen, who crossed her arms and pouted.

Jeremy continued, "We can relax and enjoy ourselves now, but I wanted to remind you that the day after tomorrow the town of Clinchport is hosting a rodeo. If some of you now expert horsemen want to try your luck at calf roping or steer wrestling—well, as part of your Wagons West experience, a local stable will provide horses to anyone who wants to give it a try." He grinned. "I would suggest first, though, that you check out what events they're having. If you still want to participate, the Rocking S stable is directly behind the west grandstand. Just

14

tell the head wrangler you're with Wagons West, and he'll help you choose a horse. Any questions?"

Karen Nicely held up her hand. "What if we don't want to ride in the rodeo? I'm still sore from riding all day on the trail."

Jeremy chuckled. "Then you can join me in the grandstand and watch while your fellow pioneers bust some broncos."

"Or some other parts of their own anatomies," Mr. Cate added with a smile.

Everyone laughed again, and then the crowd broke up. Though there would be several more hours of daylight, most people returned to their wagons. The Saddle Club, however, headed straight for the rodeo grounds.

"Let's go choose our horses first," said Stevie, pulling up the hem of her long brown pioneer dress and hurrying down the grassy slope.

"Why?" asked Lisa as she jogged along behind. "We don't even know what events they're having."

"Because if we get good horses first, we can win anything. If we sign up for the events first and wind up with plugs, then we're doomed before we've even started."

"Oh, Stevie," Carole laughed. "Only you would come up with a strategy like that."

They hurried across the large arena, which had been covered with loose, fine dirt. Though it was dusty to walk

15

on, the dirt would cushion the falls the rodeo riders took from the bucking broncos and gyrating bulls. The girls threaded their way through the west grandstand, then crossed the racetrack over to the Rocking S ranch, a long log building that had several horses tied in front.

"Howdy." A tall cowboy wearing short-fringed chaps greeted them as they entered the piney-smelling stable. "I'm Pete Parsons," he said, his thick black mustache drooping over his mouth as he talked. "Can I help you?"

"We're with Wagons West," explained Stevie, "and we'd like horses for the rodeo."

"You would, eh?" The cowboy smiled. "You ever ridden horses before?"

"Yes," replied Carole. "Back in Virginia we ride practically every day."

"And we've all ridden Western before, too," Lisa added.

"Well, then I guess you know what you're doing. Come on back here with me and I'll show you what we've got. We raise mostly quarter horses at this barn."

The girls followed Pete to a small corral behind the stable. Half a dozen muscular quarter horses grazed contentedly in the long green grass, their tails lazily swishing at the few flies that buzzed around them. About twenty feet away two other cowboys leaned against the fence, looking over the same horses. Stevie made a choking noise. One of the cowboys was Gabriel!

"I don't believe it," she muttered in frustration. "It's like wherever we go, he's there first!"

Gabriel glanced over and saw the girls. "Hi, ladies." He smiled and tipped his hat again. "Are you here to choose horses for the rodeo?"

"We are," said Stevie. "How about you?"

He nodded. "I can't decide between that sorrel with the blaze and the palomino."

"Unless you're a mighty good rider, I wouldn't choose the sorrel," the other cowboy advised. "Tumbleweed's a handful."

"Then I'll take Tumbleweed," cried Stevie, flashing a triumphant grin at Gabriel.

"Are you sure you're that good a rider, miss?" Pete Parsons frowned with concern.

"I'm sure I'm just as good as he is," Stevie replied, nodding at Gabriel.

"Hey, whatever." Gabriel shrugged. "I was going to choose the palomino, anyway. In a rodeo you need a horse you can depend on, not one that might go loco on you."

"Oh, I don't think Tumbleweed will go loco on me," Stevie assured him as she eyed the horse's powerfully built hindquarters. Tumbleweed looked at her and tossed his head as if he knew she was talking about him. "Maybe he would with someone less experienced, but I think I can handle him."

17

Pete and the other cowboy shook their heads while Lisa and Carole just rolled their eyes. A few minutes later, they decided on horses of their own—Lisa chose a tall gray horse named Ghost, and Carole decided on Pogo, a husky black-and-white pinto mare. After that the girls hurried to the arena to sign up for the events they would ride in.

"I hope they have barrel racing," said Lisa.

"Me too," Carole replied. "That's the one rodeo event we've done before."

"And we know how good we are at it," laughed Stevie.

The sign-up area was in the office under the grandstand. Various sheets of rodeo information lay on a long table. The girls studied the lists of events carefully. Everything was divided by age, and anyone between twelve and eighteen could ride in the five junior events.

"Let's see." Carole peered at the lists. "We've got barrel racing, calf roping, pole bending, goat wrestling, and a quarter-mile race."

"And a barbecue dinner with awards for the top riders afterward," Lisa read over her shoulder.

"And no all-girl cow chip tossing!" crowed Stevie. "Great!"

"What shall we sign up for?" Carole grabbed the pencil that was tied to the table and looked at her friends.

"Let's sign up for everything," suggested Stevie. "I can see the headlines now: 'Pine Hollow Riders Sweep Clinchport Rodeo!' "

Carole laughed. "Come on, Stevie, that's impossible. We can't do all five events. In the first place, we'd spend the whole day just running around the grounds, and in the second place, no single horse could do all those events. Most cowboys ride several horses in a rodeo."

"I guess you're right," Stevie agreed reluctantly.

"Let's all do barrel racing, since we're good at it, and then let's each sign up for one other event, just for fun," said Lisa. "That way we can still hang out with the pioneers some and watch the adult events."

Stevie shrugged. "Sounds good to me." She looked at the sign-up sheets. "I think I'll do barrel racing and the quarter-mile race. After all, we're riding quarter horses. That's what they were bred to do."

"Then I'll take barrel racing and pole bending." Carole laughed. "I've never bent a pole before. It should be fun."

Lisa frowned. "I guess I'll take barrel racing and goat wrestling. After wrestling with Veronica for the past week, I should be able to take care of one measly little goat."

"Well, let me tell you that goat wrestling is a little different than leading one old milk cow across the prairie," a voice said behind her. They turned to see Gabriel, smiling smugly, a lariat slung over his shoulder.

"What do you know about it?" Stevie said, crossing her arms. "How many goats have you wrestled?"

"Enough to know that you have to be fast and strong and not afraid to get dirty," snapped Gabriel. "It's a whole

19

lot different from old girly barrel racing. Anybody who's smart enough to hang on a horse could do that."

"And I guess you think we're just that smart?" Stevie asked.

Gabriel shrugged. "Maybe. I have my doubts about the other events, though. Girls always worry that they'll fall off and mess up their hair or tear their clothes or that they'll hurt their horses if they make them go fast." He snorted and shook his head. "Girls just aren't strong enough or fast enough to do well at rodeoing."

Stevie's eyes flashed. "You want to bet on that?" she cried.

"Sure," said Gabriel, his cheeks suddenly growing red. "I'll make a bet with you. We'll go one on one. You enter all five events on Tumbleweed and I'll enter all five events on my palomino, Napoleon. That way we'll find out who the better rider is once and for all."

"Hey, that's crazy," said Carole. "That's not fair to the horses. They'll be exhausted."

"Sure it is," replied Gabriel. "These aren't your pampered little English hunters. These are tough Western quarter horses."

"But wait, you guys," Lisa protested. "Remember we're on this trip to have fun and re-create some history, not kill each other at a rodeo."

Gabriel smiled at her. "Your buddy here is the one who wants to bet." He turned back to Stevie. "Well?" he asked again. "How about it?"

"You're on!" cried Stevie. She stuck out her hand to seal the bet. Gabriel shook it as Lisa and Carole looked on in horror.

"All five events on the same horse," Stevie repeated. "And may the best rider win."

"I CAN'T GET over how he thinks we're scared we'll mess up our hair!" Stevie fumed the next morning as she pulled on her regular blue jeans. The girls were dressing inside their wagon, and for the first time all week they were not putting on pioneer clothes but their everyday riding gear.

"Stevie, you need to calm down about this," said Carole. "You tossed and turned all night, always muttering something about Gabriel."

"I did not!" Stevie cried.

"Yes, you did, Stevie. I heard you." Lisa dipped her toothbrush in their bucket of water. "Just listen to yourself right now. We haven't even had breakfast yet and you're already grumbling about him."

"He is just such a jerk!" Stevie jammed her shirttail into her jeans.

"Yes, he is," Carole agreed. "But you can't let jerks talk you into doing things that are crazy and maybe dangerous. You've only been in one rodeo event in your entire life, and now you're betting that tomorrow you'll win everything from pole bending to goat wrestling. I wish you would just calm down and think about it a minute. You could get hurt doing all those things."

"I know, I know," said Stevie, raking a comb through her tousled hair. "It is crazy, but I just can't stand the idea of that nitwit guy thinking he's a better rider than me."

"Stevie, he may not be better than you, but admit it—he is an awfully good rider," Lisa said. "Remember how he jumped that horse bareback, *and* in the dark, the night of the stampede? Why don't you go find him this morning and just tell him you've changed your mind?"

"I could never do that!" Stevie said. "Anyway, he just got lucky over that fence. It wasn't all that high."

"Okay, okay." Lisa returned her toothbrush to her backpack. "I give up. Let's go eat breakfast now. We can discuss what a lucky rider Gabriel is over a nice bowl of hot mush."

A few minutes later the girls were sitting by the campfire, eating their mush. Shelly Bean had greeted them warmly as they came through the chow line, and for once Gabriel was not in sight.

"Why don't we go for a ride after breakfast?" suggested Lisa. "We need to get to know our horses before the rodeo tomorrow."

23

"Good idea," Carole said. "It'll be great to do some fun riding again. Nikkia's a good horse, but he and I mostly just plugged along with the wagon train."

Suddenly little Eileen appeared, still dressed in her pioneer outfit. "How come you're not wearing your pioneer clothes?" she demanded, her hands on her hips. "That's against the rules."

"Because we're going to be in the rodeo," explained Stevie. "You can't ride in a barrel race wearing a pioneer dress."

"I'm going to tell Jeremy!" Eileen wagged her finger at them. "It's against the rules for you not to wear pioneer clothes at all times, and it's not fair to everybody else!" With that she turned and ran toward her own wagon, shrieking for Jeremy at the top of her lungs.

Carole shook her head as she watched Eileen run away. "That kid is unbelievable."

"I feel kind of sorry for her," said Lisa. "I mean, if she's this obnoxious now, just think what she'll be like when she grows up."

"Ugh." Stevie shuddered. "I don't *even* want to think about it. Let's go ride."

They washed their breakfast dishes and headed toward the stable. They were just strolling down to the rodeo grounds when Stevie suddenly stopped. "Look!" She pointed to someone bent low over a horse that was thundering down one side of the track. "It's him! He's practicing already! He's racing the quarter-mile on Napoleon and it's barely sunup!"

Carole and Lisa looked where Stevie pointed. Sure enough, Napoleon was galloping around the track, his long flaxen tail flying in the wind.

"Do you believe that?" Stevie cried, running down the hill. "He must have started practicing at dawn!" She turned to Lisa and Carole. "Come on! There's not a moment to lose!"

The girls hurried down to the stable. Pete, the cowboy they'd met the day before, had put the horses they'd chosen in three separate stalls, so all the girls had to do was brush them and saddle them up.

"They're down thataway." Pete pointed to the left side of the stable. "And their gear is in the room next to the hayloft stairs. You'll see their names above their saddles."

"Thanks, Pete!" the girls called as they headed to their horses.

"You girls be careful." Pete looked at Stevie and frowned. "Don't use your spurs on Tumbleweed unless you want him to take off like a rocket."

"I'm going to need a rocket for that quarter-mile race," said Stevie.

Pete chuckled. "Then I think you may have gotten just what you need."

When they reached their horses, Ghost and Pogo were

busily munching hay, and Tumbleweed had stuck his head over the stall door.

"Do you think Tumbleweed might bite or kick you, Stevie?" Lisa asked.

"I don't care what he does to me," Stevie said, "as long as he wins those events."

Lisa and Carole exchanged worried frowns. Then each girl entered her horse's stall and began to get acquainted.

Stevie opened Tumbleweed's door quietly, looking down at the stable floor and speaking to him in a soft voice. She rubbed his nose only after she'd heard him give an inviting whinny, and then she looked up and smiled at him. His brown eyes seemed to twinkle back at her, and soon she was rubbing his back and legs, getting him accustomed to her touch.

"How are you doing, Stevie?" Carole called as she gave Pogo a good scratch behind the ears.

"I'm doing fine," Stevie said, gingerly lifting Tumbleweed's front hoof. "Tumbleweed seems like a real sweetheart."

"No kicking? No biting? No foaming at the mouth?" Lisa asked as she began to comb Ghost's silky gray mane.

"Not so far," Stevie replied. "Like Pete said, I guess it must be a spur thing."

"Ha, ha, ha," someone laughed outside the stalls. "Maybe it's a spur-of-the-moment thing!"

The girls looked out to see who was talking to them. A tall woman with bright red hair stood there. She wore tight-fitting jeans and a bright tie-dyed T-shirt with a green sequined vest that read "San Antonio Sal" across the front.

"Sorry," she said, grinning broadly. "I guess I couldn't resist a pun like that."

"It's okay," laughed Carole. "We're just used to Stevie being in charge of the pun department."

"Stevie?" The woman frowned.

"Yeah, me." Stevie smiled. "I'm Stevie Lake. These are my friends Carole Hanson and Lisa Atwood."

"Howdy," the woman replied. "I'm San Antonio Sal. Y'all must be here for the rodeo."

"We are," said Lisa. "We're with Wagons West."

"That's great," Sal said. "I'm here for the rodeo, too."

"Are you a rider?" Carole blinked at the wild colors of Sal's outfit.

"Shoot, no." Sal threw her head back and gave a deep belly laugh. "I gave up rodeoing years ago. Got too hard on my back, and also my backside. Now I'm a clown. Me and my partners, the Texarkana Twins, are supposed to work the junior events here tomorrow."

"Really?" Lisa's eyes grew wide. "Are the Texarkana Twins here, too?"

"Nope. They're driving up from Donnersville tonight. My horse Sadie and I came up here early, just to check things out." She grinned at the girls, whose horses were now saddled up and ready to go. "Are y'all going on a trail ride?"

27

"No," said Stevie. "We're going to the arena to practice. We've got a lot to learn and not a whole lot of time to learn it in."

"Well, don't let me keep you from your labors. Sadie and I may see you out in the ring a little later."

The girls led their horses into the arena. Gabriel was gone, so they had the place to themselves. They led each horse to the middle of the big ring and carefully mounted up. Ghost turned in a little circle when Lisa mounted, but Pogo stood quietly while Carole climbed on board. Lisa and Carole waited to see what Tumbleweed and Stevie would do.

"Here goes nothing," Stevie said, gathering her reins and planting her left foot in the stirrup.

"Good luck," Carole called.

Stevie hoisted herself up and threw her right leg over Tumbleweed. The horse stood as docilely as any of the horses did at Pine Hollow; then he arched his neck and did a little dance, as if he were eager to tackle anything Stevie might have in mind.

"I think this horse is terrific," Stevie said, giving Tumbleweed a pat on the neck. "He sure behaves for me."

"Maybe he realizes he's carrying the Amazon warrior queen of the West," Lisa said, chuckling.

"You can laugh now," said Stevie, "but you're going to love it when I beat Gabriel in all five events tomorrow!"

"Well, let's see what these guys can do," said Carole, urging Pogo into a trot.

They warmed up in the arena, practicing their lopes and turns and lead changes. All three of the horses had the surefootedness quarter horses are known for, and all seemed to be willing and responsive mounts.

"I think we chose pretty well." Carole pulled up in the center of the ring to give Pogo a breather.

"Me too," said Lisa. "Ghost is a super horse!"

"Hi, everybody!" a voice called from the sideline. "Y'all look pretty good out there!"

The girls turned. San Antonio Sal loped toward them, riding a beautiful leopard-spotted Appaloosa. "I believe you must have ridden once or twice before," she said, pulling up beside them.

"Well, yes, we do ride a lot." Carole smiled, pleased that Sal could see they weren't total tenderfeet.

"Practically every day," added Stevie.

Sal pushed her bright orange cowboy hat back on her head. "I can tell. All of you ride wonderfully well. What events are you doing in the rodeo?"

The girls looked at each other. "Well, Carole and I are just doing two each," Lisa said. "Stevie's going to be in all five."

"All five?" Sal's eyebrows shot up in surprise as she looked at Stevie. "Have you ever done all five of these events before?"

"No," Stevie admitted sheepishly. "But I believe you can do anything you want to if you want to bad enough."

"This boy on our wagon train, our assistant trail boss,

thinks men can do everything better than women," Carole explained. "He sort of dared Stevie to compete in all five events."

"I see," Sal said thoughtfully. She looked at Stevie, then grinned. "Well, good for you, girl. I say go get 'em! You'll just have to show that boy whose hog ate the cabbage!"

"You don't know anything about pole bending, do you?" Stevie asked.

Sal laughed. "Why, I sure do. Pole bending is just riding in and out around a string of poles stuck in the ground. Riders as good as you won't have a bit of trouble with pole bending if you remember one thing: Straighten up in the saddle a little bit as you go around the poles. That way you won't unbalance your horse when he's doing all those flying lead changes."

Stevie looked puzzled.

"Look." Sal pointed to the middle of the arena. "Just pretend there are about six poles lined up over there and watch what I do."

The girls watched as Sal turned Sadie straight down the middle of the arena. "Okay," she called. "Somebody say go and I'll pretend I'm pole bending."

"Go!" said Carole.

Suddenly Sadie leaped forward at a full gallop. Twenty feet later she made a quick curve to the right; twenty feet after that, a quick curve to the left. San Antonio Sal was weaving through a pole bending course without a pole in

30

sight. At the end of the arena, Sadie made a sharp half turn and they zigzagged back up to the girls.

"Wheee!" Sal let go of her reins and lifted her arms high above her head as she and Sadie roared past them. "I won!"

"Wow!" said Lisa. "That was incredible!"

"Oh, well, it wasn't much." Sal rode back around and looked at Stevie. "Did you see what I meant, though, about leaning back when your horse makes his turn? They're twisting and lead changing so hard and fast they appreciate anything you can do to keep them balanced."

"Gosh," Stevie said. "Thanks. Now at least I'll know what I'm supposed to do."

"Hey, I was going to ask you girls if you wanted to ride out in the country with me and Sadie. I haven't been up here in years, and I'd kind of like to see how the landscape's changed."

"Sure," said Carole. "I'd love to go."

"Me too." Lisa gave Ghost a pat. "Stevie? How about you?"

"Oh, I think I'll stay here and work on my pole bending. If Gabriel was out here practicing, then I feel like that's what I'd better be doing, too. You guys go on ahead. I'll do a trail ride later."

"Are you sure?" Carole frowned. Normally Stevie was the first one to suggest a trail ride.

"Sure I'm sure. Tumbleweed and I will stay here and practice our flying lead changes."

31

"Okay." Carole and Pogo trotted after the others. "See you later."

Stevie watched as her friends rode out of the arena. As much as she wanted to go with them, the only thing she could think about right then was Gabriel, and the whole idea of him made her mad. *How could someone so obnoxious and annoying grab so much of my attention?* she asked herself. Maybe it was because they'd lived so close together these past few days. *Maybe whoever you live close to could just take over your brain, and I just had the bad luck to get stuck with Gabriel.* She pulled a knot out of Tumbleweed's mane and frowned. *But if obnoxious Gabriel's taken over my mind, then who's taken over Phil's? What if there's a girl he's living close to who's smart and funny and likes the outdoors? Somebody like that could really take over someone's brain!* Stevie shook her head. She couldn't allow herself to think about that right then. She had twenty-four hours to get ready for five different rodeo events.

"Come on, Tumbleweed," she said. She clucked to the horse and headed toward the spot where Sal had given her demonstration. "We need to bend some imaginary poles, and we need to bend them fast!"

4

BY THE TIME Shelly Bean clanged the triangle for lunch, Stevie had finished her first practice with Tumbleweed. She cooled him down and returned him to his stall, then hurried back to the wagon train to eat with her friends. She found Lisa and Carole sitting under a tree, just finishing their lunch of stewed apples and potato pancakes.

"Grab a plate, Stevie, and join us," Lisa called, looking up from the notebook she was writing in.

Stevie hurried through the chow line and sat down just as her friends were filling in some details of the journal they were keeping for Deborah.

"You and Tumbleweed must have had quite a practice," said Carole, noticing Stevie's sweaty face.

"We did," replied Stevie as she took her first bite of pancake. "He's a great little horse." She grinned. "And I just know he's a whole lot faster than Napoleon."

Carole and Lisa glanced at each other. They were growing tired of Stevie's obsession with Gabriel, and neither wanted to spoil their lunch break by discussing it. "You know, we need to write some things about San Antonio Sal in here," Lisa said. "She's the first rodeo clown I've ever met."

"Me too," said Carole. "Write down all that stuff she told us about clowning—about how each clown has her own clown personality and each of them can do special tricks."

Lisa nodded as she made notes. "And all of them have to entertain the audience as well as help the riders get out of the ring safely. It must be hard work.

"San Antonio Sal's so funny," Lisa continued. "I can't wait to meet the Texarkana Twins. They must really be a hoot."

"I know." Carole giggled. "Remember all those jokes she told us about rodeo cowboys?"

Lisa nodded with a grin. Both girls waited for Stevie, who loved jokes above all else, to ask to hear one, but she remained silent, just picking at her lunch and gazing over at the rodeo arena.

"Hello?" Carole reached over and tapped Stevie on her knee. "Carole to Stevie. Joke alert! You're about to miss some good ones!"

"Huh?" Stevie looked up as if she hadn't heard a word they'd said.

"Stevie, you've got to get a grip on this!" Lisa cried. "Gabriel is just one know-it-all, arrogant guy. You're letting this competition with him take over your life!"

Stevie blinked. "Gabriel?"

"Yes. Gabriel," said Carole. "He's all you've thought about since you two made that silly bet."

"No, he's not." Stevie shook her head. "I wasn't thinking about him at all just then."

"All right, then what were you thinking about?" asked Lisa. "What has got you so deep in thought that you didn't even hear someone talking about some terrific jokes they just heard?"

"Oh, it's not important." Embarrassed, Stevie looked down at her plate.

Carole frowned again. "Of course it's important, Stevie, if it's zoning you out to Mars. Just tell us what it is. Remember, we're The Saddle Club. We're duty bound to help."

Stevie blinked at her last bite of apple. "I was just thinking about Phil," she finally admitted with a sigh.

"Phil?" Carole and Lisa looked at each other in astonishment. "What about Phil?"

Stevie sighed. "Oh, just that ever since I've been stuck here with that twerp Gabriel, Phil's probably been rafting down the river with some pretty neat girl. I bet he's met someone who's prettier than me and smarter than me and more fun than me," she said miserably.

"Oh, Stevie, that's just not possible," said Lisa. "Phil likes you more than anybody. You two make a perfect couple."

"We did until we took these separate vacations. Now every night he's probably dreaming about some cute girl on his raft who looks terrific in a swimsuit and paddles like a pro!"

"Stevie, I don't think Phil would fall head over heels in love with a totally new person that fast," reasoned Carole. "After all, his days must be pretty busy, too, if he's navigating a white-water river and camping in a different place every night. He's probably too tired to even think about anything romantic!"

"I don't know," Stevie muttered, remembering her own unwelcome dreams about Gabriel. "Phil's got a lot of energy."

"Did I overhear someone talking about energy?"

The girls looked over their shoulders. Gabriel stood there grinning, his cowboy hat pushed back on his head at a rakish angle.

"Actually, you were overhearing a private conversation," Lisa told him stiffly.

"Sorry," he said. "I didn't mean to intrude. I just saw Stevie practicing her pole bending and wondered how Tumbleweed was working out for her."

"Fine," answered Stevie, turning to face him. "He's a great horse. One of the fastest I've ever ridden."

Gabriel laughed. "That may be, but he looks like a real nag next to Napoleon."

Stevie narrowed her eyes. "You know, a horse is only half the team. You've got to be a darn good rider to know how to use one."

"Absolutely," Gabriel agreed. "Particularly in calf roping. I was the junior county champion calf roper in my state last year."

"Oh, really?" said Stevie. "I was the junior champion barrel racer of the Bar None riders last year."

"That's pretty good, for a girly sport like barrel racing," Gabriel said. "Are you any good at goat wrestling?"

Stevie tossed her head. "Of course I'm good at goat wrestling. I can pin a goat to the ground in eight seconds flat."

"Oh?" Gabriel raised one eyebrow. "Would you like to bet on that?"

"Sure," Stevie replied. "What'll it be?"

Lisa and Carole looked at each other in horror. To their knowledge, Stevie had never touched a goat, let alone wrestled one, in her life.

Gabriel spoke quickly. "Let's say that if you pin a goat in eight seconds flat, you get to make me perform any dare of your choice. If you can't, then I get to make you do any dare of my choice."

37

"Oh, make it more interesting than that," said Stevie, faking a yawn.

"Okay." Gabriel leaned back and stuck his thumbs in the belt loops of his jeans. "How about, whoever does better in the whole rodeo gets to make the loser perform one super dare of their choice? All five events. No holds barred, no questions asked."

"You're on!" Stevie leaped to her feet and again stuck out her hand. "Shake on it!"

"So much for trying to get her interested in rodeo clowns!" Lisa whispered to Carole as Gabriel and Stevie shook hands.

After they had sealed their wager, Gabriel tipped his hat to the girls and strolled whistling toward the arena.

"Why are you two looking at me like that?" Stevie asked when she turned back to her friends.

"Stevie, how many goats have you wrestled in your life?" Carole asked.

"Well, none," Stevie confessed. "I fudged a little on that one. But how hard can it be? I've wrestled my brothers, and they all smell like goats."

"And how many calves have you roped and poles have you bent, Miss Champion Barrel Racer of the Bar None Riders?" Lisa questioned her further.

"Not too many," admitted Stevie.

"Almost none," corrected Carole. "And you weren't the champion barrel racer of the Bar None Ranch, either. Kate was!"

"Okay, so I stretched the truth a little."

Carole frowned. "Stevie, I'm getting really worried about you."

"Why?" Stevie looked puzzled.

"Because you haven't been this competitive in a long time, and it seems to be taking over every moment of your life. You're bragging about things that aren't true, and you're not even enjoying our trip anymore because of this competition." Carole shook her head. "Plus, who knows what a jerk like Gabriel might make you do if he wins the bet?"

"Yeah," agreed Lisa. "It might be something really humiliating!"

"But you two are assuming he's going to win," Stevie replied. "He's not. I am. Don't worry about what he might make me do. Help me think up some appropriately disgusting thing I can make him do!"

"I don't know, Stevie." Carole frowned. "He's had a lot more experience at these rodeo events than you."

"Yoo-hoo! Girls!" Another voice rang out. "I've been looking all over the place for you three!"

The girls turned again. San Antonio Sal was hurrying up to their spot beneath the tree, clutching a sheet of white paper.

"I'm so glad I found you!" she said breathlessly. "I've got a real emergency on my hands!"

"What's wrong?" Lisa asked quickly.

Sal waved the sheet of paper at the girls. "This is a

message the lady down at the rodeo office took for me. The Texarkana Twins just called from Donnersville. They ate a whole mess of bad catfish last night and came down with food poisoning. They're not going to be able to make the rodeo!"

"Oh no!" cried Carole. "We really wanted to meet them."

"Well, that's not the worst part. All sanctioned rodeo events must have a team of three clowns. I've called every clown within two hundred miles and they're all booked for bigger rodeos. If I can't find two replacements by tomorrow, the junior events will have to be canceled!"

"That's terrible!" Lisa exclaimed.

"Well, that's where I was wondering if maybe you girls could help me out. I've seen how well all three of you ride, and you seem to have a lot of good old-fashioned cow sense about you. Would you be willing to take over the Texarkana Twins' part of the act? I could show you the routines and teach you how to do the makeup. Plus, we'll be working the junior events, so you won't be contending with any wild broncs or bulls." Sal smiled hopefully. "Course, it will mean you won't be able to compete, since you'll be working the whole time."

"Count me in!" cried Carole. "I can ride in a junior rodeo some other time, but I'll probably never get the chance to be a rodeo clown again!"

"Me too," said Lisa. "Especially if without us, the junior events will be canceled."

Everyone looked at Stevie, waiting for her to join them. "I don't know," she finally mumbled, frowning.

"Stevie, how can you not say yes?" Lisa asked. "It's what The Saddle Club is supposed to do! Help out at all times!"

"I know," said Stevie. "And if you and Carole weren't here I'd certainly do it. But since you two are here and you're such good riders, you really don't need me." She took a deep breath and looked at San Antonio Sal. "I hope you'll understand, but I'd rather compete in the events this time. I know Carole and Lisa will do a great job helping you out."

Carole's and Lisa's faces fell, but San Antonio Sal gave Stevie a big wink.

"That's okay, Stevie. I understand. I think you've got something to prove tomorrow, and with the help of your friends here, you'll still have the opportunity to prove it."

Sal turned to Carole and Lisa. "Okay, girls. My trailer's parked beneath the west grandstand. After you finish your lunch, come on down there and we'll get to work. By tomorrow afternoon you two will be real live rodeo clowns!"

5

"WHY, HELLO THERE, Stevie," Pete Parsons called as Stevie walked into the cool dimness of the Rocking S stable. "I thought you were done riding for the day."

She looked around. Pete sat on a bale of hay, twirling a small lasso in a crazy-looking circle.

Stevie smiled and shook her head. "No, Pete, I'm nowhere near done for the day. In fact, I think I probably should have skipped lunch and just stayed on Tumbleweed."

Pete effortlessly spun the lasso out in a wide figure eight. "How so? Did you get so tired of driving that old Conestoga wagon that now you're hankering to spend all day in the saddle?"

"No. It's a lot more serious than that."

"What do you mean?" Pete quit spinning the rope and looked at her.

Stevie told him the story of Gabriel and his superior attitude and how he thought he was a much better rider than she was and how they had a bet going to settle it once and for all.

"You know, I wondered if that boy wasn't acting a little too big for his britches when he first came in here." Pete frowned and stroked his thick black mustache. "But I watched you on Tumbleweed. You're a good enough rider to beat him."

"I know I can beat him in the quarter-mile race and the barrel racing," said Stevie. "But I have my doubts about those other events."

"Oh, you're probably just a little rusty. It'll all come back to you when the chutes open."

Stevie shook her head. "No, Pete, you don't understand. I only learned how to pole bend this morning, and I've never roped a calf in a rodeo or wrestled a goat in my life!"

Pete's brown eyes widened. "You've never roped any calves? Nor wrestled one goat in your entire life?" He moved the piece of straw he was chewing from one corner of his mouth to the other and frowned at Stevie.

"I've never roped in a competition, and I haven't done any roping at all in a while," Stevie answered honestly.

"Well," he said, gathering up his rope and unfolding

himself from the bale of hay, "that's a horse of a different color. I guess we'd better get busy. You need some emergency rodeo training, and you need it pronto!"

"Wow!" Carole breathed as she and Lisa stepped inside San Antonio Sal's trailer. "This is the most fabulous place I've ever seen!"

The girls looked around the small, colorful room. Every inch was covered with clown equipment. The floor was lined with all sorts of purple and green wigs on stands, and boxes overflowed with polka-dot parasols, water-squirting flowers, and rubber chickens. A large, brightly lit mirror hung on one wall between two clothes racks, where baggy, oversized pants dangled next to sequined vests and crazy tie-dyed blouses.

Lisa blinked at the bright, glittery colors. "I've never seen so many spangles and sparkles and sequins in my life!"

"Well, it ain't much, but it's home." San Antonio Sal chuckled. "Y'all sit down here and we'll get to work."

The girls sat down in front of the mirror. Sal pulled out one huge makeup kit full of greasepaint and charcoal pencils, then another one with fake noses and floppy false ears and fuzzy stick-on eyebrows.

"Let's invent your personalities first," she said, uncapping a tube of clear face cream. "Then you'll know what kind of clown to be."

"What do you mean?" Carole asked.

"Well, if you draw on a sad face, then your clown moves are going to be slower and your body language will be more droopy." Sal squirted out some cream for Lisa. "If you put on a goofy face, then you'll clown in a looser, less controlled way."

"Oh, I think I'll be goofy," giggled Lisa, rubbing the cream onto her face. "I'd never get the chance to do that at home."

"What if you just want to be happy?" Carole asked Sal.

"Happy's probably the best face to put on," Sal said. "That way you can be anything—mad, sad, goofy—according to what goes on in the ring."

"What are you?" asked Lisa.

"I'm always happy," answered Sal. "Texarkana Cindy's usually goofy, while Texarkana Ruth's usually mad. It works out pretty well for us in the ring."

"Wow." Lisa looked at all the tubes of greasepaint scattered in front of Sal's mirror. "There are so many possibilities."

Sal laughed. "That's what makes clowning such a wonderful life. Every day you can be somebody different, and every day you get to make people laugh. Sometimes you even get to save a cowboy's life." She rummaged through a drawer under the table and pulled out a book. "Here's an album of clown face designs. Look through there and maybe you can get some ideas."

Carole giggled as she and Lisa turned the pages of the

clown book. "I wonder if Stevie's having this much fun," she whispered.

"TWIRL, TWIRL, TWIRL, TWIRL, throw!" Stevie said to herself as she swung the lasso. She was practicing her cattle roping at a target Pete had rigged up for her—a plastic calf's head stuck in a bale of hay. She swung the lasso one final time, then let it go. The loop soared through the air, only to fall harmlessly to the ground a foot away from the plastic head.

"Darn!" she said, dismounting for the twentieth time. "This isn't working and I'm doing everything just like I'm supposed to!"

Disgustedly she re-coiled the lasso and walked back to Tumbleweed. There was a sympathetic look in the horse's eyes, as if he wished he could do something to help her. She rubbed his neck. "Maybe we should take a break," she said. "My right arm feels like it's on fire from all this roping."

She grabbed Tumbleweed's reins and led him to a tall cottonwood tree that grew at one end of the corral. For the past three hours she had practiced what Pete had shown her—everything from tightening the noose of a rope to fit over a calf's head to learning how to lean low in the saddle before she started to tackle a goat. As nearly as she could tell, the only progress she had made was to irritate her aching hands and make her rear end even sorer than it had been when she was driving the wagon.

"I don't know, Tumbleweed," she said softly as the sturdy little horse took long swallows of water from the trough. "I've done this before, but I'm really out of practice. This time I might have seriously overestimated my talents as a cowgirl."

"Hi!" said a familiar voice behind her. She knew without looking that it was Gabriel.

"Hi," she answered, quickly rearranging her expression from dismay into confidence. She grinned broadly. "How's it going?"

"Great," he said, leaning against the top rail of the fence. He'd changed into a shirt that made his eyes look even bluer than they normally did. He nodded at the plastic calf's head protruding from the bale of hay and smiled. "Need a little practice, huh?"

Stevie shrugged. "I was just testing out Tumbleweed. I'm in great shape."

"I see," said Gabriel. He dangled one end of the rope he held in his hands and looked at the ground. "You know, I've been thinking about this bet we've got going."

"Oh?" Stevie's heart began to beat faster. Maybe Gabriel was about to chicken out.

"Yeah. In fact, I've been thinking about it all day."

Stevie smiled to herself. He was trying to find a way to weasel out of it! Maybe there was a chance they could forget this whole thing and she could get back to having some fun with Lisa and Carole. "And?" she asked hopefully.

47

"And I've just decided what I'm going to make you do when I win!" he announced gleefully.

"When you *win?*" she repeated as she felt her face heat up with both anger and disappointment.

"Yeah. When I win." He looked at her and smiled. "It's really going to be great! Everybody's going to love it!"

"Oh, really? What is it?" Stevie asked in spite of herself.

"Are you kidding?" He laughed and tilted his hat back on his head. "Do you honestly think I'd tell you beforehand? Forget it! That's for me to know and you to find out!"

"Well, before you start enjoying your little dare too much, you'd better start worrying about what I'm going to make you do when *I* win," retorted Stevie quickly. "It'll go down in the annals of rodeo history! And I'm not telling you, either!"

"Fine!" said Gabriel.

"Fine!" Stevie cried back, watching with clenched fists as he slung his rope over his shoulder and sauntered off toward the stable. She snorted. Gabriel was undoubtedly the most impossible person she'd ever met, and now she was involved in a bet with him she couldn't get out of!

"Come on, Tumbleweed," she said, leading the horse back to the plastic calf head after Gabriel was out of sight. "Now not only do we have to win, we have to think up some totally disgusting thing for him to do!" She looked at the horse and gave a grim smile. "But we'll do it, even if we have to practice all night!"

IN THE RODEO arena, three clowns were rolling out a dented barrel. One clown was tall, with bright red hair and a sequined vest. The other two were shorter. One wore a baggy black suit and a derby along with a red nose and candy-striped socks, while the other sported a frizzy green wig with pointed Martian ears and an old-timey long-sleeved purple bathing suit.

"I must say, y'all look just as good as the Texarkana Twins," Sal laughed as Lisa and Carole helped her maneuver the barrel out into the arena.

"Well, I feel pretty happy." Carole laughed and pulled up one of her striped socks.

"And I certainly feel goofy." Lisa adjusted the green wig on her head.

"Great. Just keep those feelings in mind while I show you our routines. That way everything will go perfectly."

Sal stood the barrel up on one end. It was lightweight but deep enough for a person to squeeze inside. "Let me give you a brief course in rodeo clowning. If you've ever noticed before, rodeo clowns usually work in teams of three. We have a bullfighter, a point clown, and a barrel man. The bullfighter is a clown who jumps around and tries to distract the bull after the rider's off his back. You have to be nimble and quick to be a bullfighter."

"And brave, too," added Carole.

"Absolutely," Sal agreed. She thumped the barrel. "The barrel man stays inside here and watches the bullfighter work. If the bullfighter is having trouble with a bull, he leads him over to the barrel man, who stands up inside the barrel and draws the bull over to him. Then the barrel man scrunches down inside in case the bull decides the barrel would make good target practice for his horns." Sal laughed and pointed to a large dent on one side of her barrel. "That was put there by a bull named Percy who just didn't like the color of my wig one day."

"What does the point clown do?" asked Lisa.

"The point clown coordinates everybody else. If she sees the bullfighter needs help, she goes there; if the barrel man's getting tossed around too much, she helps out there. If everything's going okay, the point clown entertains the audience."

"That sounds like the toughest job of all," said Carole.

"Oh, they're all tough in their own ways, but they're also a lot of fun." Sal noticed Lisa's wary expression. "Anyway, we'll be working the junior events, so we won't have any broncs or bulls to worry about. Just calves and goats." She laughed. "They're not real strong, but they can be slippery little devils."

She banged on the barrel. "Okay. Who wants to be the barrel man? Or should I say barrel girl?"

Lisa shrugged. "I'll give it a try."

"Great," Sal said. "Hop right in there and Carole and I

will roll you around the arena. We can work on our routines as we go along."

Lisa squirmed down into the barrel.

"Are you ready?" said Sal.

"Ready!" called Lisa.

"Okay, then, clowns. Let's go!"

AS THE PURPLE evening shadows grew long over the corral, Stevie's lasso finally fell exactly over the calf's head.

"All right!" she cried as she wearily climbed off Tumbleweed. "After about a hundred throws, I finally got him!" She sighed as she loosened the rope from the plastic head. It was getting too dark to practice anymore, and she knew she was still far from good.

"Okay," she said to herself. "I may not win the calf roping, but if I'm lucky, at least I won't totally disgrace myself." She re-coiled the rope, then started to walk Tumbleweed back to the barn. The setting sun turned the filmy clouds a brilliant shade of orange.

"I wonder if Phil is having as pretty a sunset as we are?" Stevie asked aloud as Tumbleweed clopped along behind her. "I wonder if he's toasting marshmallows around a campfire or strumming a guitar or skipping rocks across a river?" She felt a sharp pang in her stomach as she imagined Phil with a new girl by his side. She would enjoy doing all the things Phil liked to do, and they would be sitting side by side every day, telling each other jokes, holding hands when the river was calm and paddling furiously through the rapids together, all the while gazing into each other's eyes.

"And here I am, alone in the middle of a dusty corral, throwing a rope around a plastic calf head," Stevie moaned. "I'm dirty and I'm sore and now I'll probably lose the rodeo tomorrow and then I'll have to do some stupid, humiliating thing that Gabriel dreamed up!

"Oh, Tumbleweed," she sighed, reaching up to rub the horse behind one of his soft ears. "How do I get into such messes?"

6

"THIS IS THE first soft thing we've sat on in over a week!" Lisa exclaimed, nestling into the old movie theater seat. "It almost seems like we're back in civilization again."

"I know," Carole said. "Feels good, doesn't it?"

"It sure does." Lisa laughed. "Particularly after spending most of the afternoon rolling around in a barrel. I feel like I've been launched into outer space!"

The girls were attending, along with all the other pioneers, a prerodeo talent show put on by the people of Clinchport. An old theater on the town square had been made into an auditorium, and the seats were filling up fast. When the houselights blinked three times, everyone realized the show was about to start.

"But you've got to admit clowning was fun," Carole

said. "I mean, putting on all that crazy makeup and then learning how to do those tricks with the horses. This was one of the neatest days I've ever had!"

Lisa and Carole giggled, then turned to Stevie. "How did your day go, Stevie?" Lisa asked. "We saw you practicing hard for the goat wrestling when we went to get Sal's bull barrel."

"Huh?" Stevie turned her gaze away from the hay bales that decorated each corner of the old stage and looked at her friends.

"I said, how did your day go?" Lisa repeated.

"Oh, great." Stevie rubbed her right shoulder as if it were sore. "After I practiced what San Antonio Sal told me about pole bending, Pete from the stable helped me with the other events. I worked on my dismounts in goat wrestling for most of the afternoon. Then I finished up by perfecting my lasso release for calf roping."

"Gosh, Stevie," said Carole. "That sounds like something my dad would dream up for his new Marine recruits. You should have joined us and had some fun learning how to clown."

"Yeah." Lisa looked at Stevie with concern. "It doesn't sound like you had nearly as much fun as we did."

"Oh, I'll have my fun tomorrow," Stevie promised with a wicked grin, "when I win the rodeo and that creep Gabriel has to do the dare of my choice." She frowned. "What do you think of making him put on my old pioneer dress and do 'women's work' for a day?"

Carole laughed. "For Gabriel, I think that would be a fate worse than death!"

"Hi, girls," someone called. They looked toward the stage. Bouncing on the seat in front of them was Eileen, her blond ponytail flying in the air with every bounce.

"You'd better stop, Eileen," Lisa warned. "You're going to break that seat."

"You can't make me!" retorted Eileen. "Nobody can make me do anything!"

"Probably not," Carole agreed with a sigh. She turned back to Stevie and Lisa. "Anyway, Stevie, guess what we learned to do with the horses today—"

"I know a secret!" Eileen blurted out in a singsongy voice.

Stevie and Lisa ignored her as Carole told about the fun they'd had learning Sal's fall-asleep-on-your-horse routine.

"I said, I know a secret!" Eileen jumped harder on the seat and singsonged even more loudly.

"Okay, Eileen." Stevie frowned at her. "So you know a secret. Good for you."

"No, I know a really *big* secret!" Eileen insisted. "One that you probably would just love to know yourself!"

Just as Stevie was about to tell Eileen to sit down and be quiet, the houselights dimmed. "Ladies and gentlemen," a voice announced over a loudspeaker. "The people of Clinchport proudly present the Clinchport High School Drill Team!"

The red velvet curtains opened. Three rows of high-school girls marched onto the stage. Some carried white rifles on their shoulders, while others waved American flags. They marched around the stage in a close-order drill to a recording of "Stars and Stripes Forever." Everyone began to clap in time to the music, and for once Eileen had to be quiet.

Three hours later the talent show was over and the girls slowly walked back to their wagon.

"That was fun, wasn't it?" said Lisa. "Those cowboys who yodeled were terrific."

Carole nodded and laughed. "They were. And I really loved the guy who danced with the pig."

"Wasn't he cool?" Stevie giggled in agreement. "That would be a terrific thing for me to make Gabriel do."

"Stevie, did you sit through that whole show just thinking about what hideous dare you could dream up for Gabriel?" Carole asked.

"Well, not the whole show," said Stevie. "Just a few parts of it. And they gave me some wonderful ideas!"

The girls got back to their wagon and pulled their sleeping bags out into the cool night air. Carole found a soft patch of ground under a tree, and soon all three of them had snuggled down for the night.

"Good night, everybody," yawned Lisa.

"Good night, Texarkana Lisa," Carole replied. "Good night, Stevie, queen of the rodeo."

"Good night, you guys."

Stevie rolled over on her side and fell into a deep sleep. At first she did not dream at all; then she began to have weird visions of horses and goats and dancing pigs. At one point Carole and Lisa floated across her dream sky in their clown costumes, while in another dream her brother Chad kept holding up a valentine heart and laughing at her. In her longest dream she and Phil were out in the desert on horseback. They were getting ready to run a quarter-mile race. San Antonio Sal stood at the starting line with a pistol in her hand, while Gabriel waited by the finish line on Stevie's side of the track.

Across from Gabriel stood a girl with beautiful green eyes and golden-red hair, smiling and waving at Phil. Phil blew her a kiss, then turned to Stevie. "That's Meghan," he said dreamily. "She speaks fluent Italian, she won a full scholarship to Harvard when she was in the sixth grade, and she plays polo." Phil smiled and patted his horse's neck. "She even loaned me her horse to ride." Stevie looked down at Phil's horse. It was a huge bay stallion that tossed his head and snorted fire. Stevie saw the name *Secretariat* stitched on his red sequined saddle pad.

"Meghan owns Secretariat?" Stevie heard her own voice come out in a mousy squeak. Phil grinned and nodded. "She's rich, too."

"Uh-huh." Stevie blinked and looked down at her mount. It was not Tumbleweed she was on, or her own

57

horse, Belle. Stevie was getting ready for a race against Secretariat on Nero, the oldest, most decrepit gelding in Pine Hollow!

"Wait!" she cried, her words seeming to come out in slow motion. "That's not fair! You can't expect Nero to keep up with Secretariat!"

Phil shrugged. Then it was too late. San Antonio Sal fired the starting gun, and Phil and the big bay stallion bounded off in a cloud of dust.

"No!" Stevie cried. "Wait! It's not fair!"

She sat up and opened her eyes, fully expecting to see Phil and Secretariat disappearing before her. Instead she saw Mr. Cate, struggling to get his water bucket back inside his wagon.

"I'm sorry if we woke you up!" he called in a hoarse whisper. He started to laugh. "Mrs. Cate kicked the bucket in her sleep and knocked it out of the wagon!"

"It's okay," Stevie whispered back, grateful to have been awakened from her nightmare. "It didn't bother me a bit."

Stevie tried to catch her breath as Mr. Cate climbed back inside his wagon. She rubbed her eyes and looked up at the million twinkling stars overhead. Though she knew a part of her was being crazy and irrational about Phil and his new girlfriend, it seemed as if that part was taking over the other, more normal parts of her. Not only did she worry about them during the day, but now they were showing up in her dreams at night!

Maybe this is some kind of ESP, she thought with alarm as she gazed up at the stars. *Maybe my dreams are trying to prepare me for the worst. Maybe there really is a girl with golden-red hair whom Phil has fallen in love with!*

She sat up straighter and shook her head. *You have no proof of that*, she lectured herself firmly. *You don't even know if any girls are on Phil's trip in the first place. And if there are any, you don't know that they're cute. And you certainly don't know that Phil has fallen in love with any of them. All you have is a bunch of feelings and dreams and worries.*

She looked over at Lisa and Carole, who were sleeping soundly, then settled back down in her sleeping bag. "Even if he has fallen in love with some wonderful red-headed girl, there's nothing I can do about it tonight," she sighed. "The best thing for me to do right now is to try to get some sleep. There's a big rodeo tomorrow, and I've got to win it!"

"I CAN'T FIND MY green wig!" Lisa cried. She stood in the middle of the wagon dressed in her long purple bathing suit, a puzzled expression on her face.

"Look outside, in that plastic storage box Sal gave us," said Carole, who was pulling up her red-and-white-striped socks.

"Good idea."

"But watch out for Stevie's lasso," Carole called as Lisa jumped out of the wagon. "She's practicing her releases."

Suddenly Carole heard a shriek and a thud. She scrambled to the open end of the wagon and looked out. Lisa sat on the ground, a tangle of rope draped around her arms and shoulders.

"Lisa! Are you okay?" Stevie hurried over to her friend.

"I'm so sorry! I was aiming at the bucket on the back of the wagon! I'd just thrown the rope when you came out!"

"I'm okay," Lisa said as Stevie untangled the rope from around her. "Just as long as you didn't mistake me for a cow!"

Stevie laughed and helped Lisa to her feet. "I don't know too many cows that come to the rodeo dressed in purple long johns!"

"Is everyone all right?" Carole asked.

"We're fine," Stevie and Lisa replied.

"I saw what you did to her!" a smaller voice called. Eileen stood beside the wagon, dressed in her pioneer costume, her hair now in pigtails.

"Oh, buzz off, Eileen," said Lisa as she began to rummage in the big plastic box for her wig. "Stevie didn't do anything to me. It was an accident."

"You don't know that for sure," Eileen snapped back.

"Hey, Eileen, why aren't you dressed for the rodeo?" Stevie asked as she re-coiled her rope. "I thought you were doing some bull riding today."

"Not me!" cried Eileen, her green eyes wide. "I would never do anything that dirty and dusty and dangerous!" She watched Stevie as she began to twirl her rope again. "Anyway, I know a secret that's a lot more fun than riding any stupid bull!"

"Really?" Stevie aimed her lasso at the wagon wheel. The noose fell around it cleanly on the first try. Stevie pulled the rope taut, then gathered it up and started all over again.

Eileen smiled coyly. "Yes. It's about two people you know really well."

"You don't say?" This time Stevie turned her attention to the parking brake at the front of the wagon. She made the noose smaller, then twirled the lasso over her head and let go. Again the noose hit its target dead on.

"Yes," Eileen said smugly. "And one of them has blue eyes."

"No kidding?" Stevie walked to the parking brake and loosened her rope. "Gosh, I wonder how many blue-eyed people might be on this wagon train. Ten? Twenty?" She turned and studied Eileen for a long moment. Slowly she started to twirl the rope again. "You know what we do with people who keep secrets around here?" she asked with a menacing grin.

"What?" Eileen stuck out her chest and tried to look fearless.

"We rope 'em." Stevie raised the lariat over her head and twirled it faster and faster. "And then we hog-tie 'em and hitch 'em to the back of the wagon and let Yankee and Doodle pull 'em around the camp until they beg for mercy!"

"No-o-o-o!" Eileen gave a thin little scream and ran off toward her parents' campsite.

"What was that noise?" Carole jumped out of the wagon, dressed in her clown costume.

Stevie chuckled. "That was the sound of a terrified Eileen."

"What happened? Did she lose her teddy bear again?" Carole asked with a frown.

"No," Stevie replied. "She was running away so that I wouldn't rope and hog-tie her and let the horses drag her around the camp."

"Stevie, did you say something to upset the poor little dear?" Carole could barely contain a laugh.

"Well, maybe a little something," Stevie admitted. Then she remembered all the trouble Eileen had caused everyone in general and herself in particular. "But it was nothing she didn't deserve," she added.

"Hey, Carole, are you ready to go?" Lisa asked, finally pulling the green wig out of the box and fitting it on her head. "Since we're going to have to put on our faces in Sal's trailer, we should get a move on."

"I'm ready." Carole adjusted her derby to just the right angle and gave her candy-striped hose a final tug. "Stevie, are you coming with us?"

"You two go ahead," said Stevie. "I'm going to practice my roping a little longer. I'll catch up with you at the arena before everything begins."

"Okay," said Carole as she and Lisa began to walk toward the rodeo grounds. "We'll see you later."

Stevie smiled as she watched the purple clown with green hair and the baggy-suited clown in a derby run down the grassy hillside. Then she went back inside the wagon and pulled out her journal. She and Phil were each keeping a diary of their trip to share when they got home, but she'd been too busy to write anything in hers since she'd been practicing for the rodeo. Now she wanted to jot down all the details of the past two days before she forgot them. Hurriedly she scribbled about the bet she'd made with Gabriel, how hard she'd been practicing for the rodeo, and how Lisa and Carole were learning to be clowns. *They are having a lot of fun*, she wrote, then looked up from her paper.

"I wonder what Phil's writing in his journal," she said aloud. She frowned, remembering her dream about Secretariat and Phil and the girl with golden-red hair. "He's probably writing about rafting down some river with this beautiful girl. She's whispering in his ear in Italian, and he's probably asked her to be his date for the big Halloween dance at school next fall." Tears began to fill Stevie's eyes. She looked at the lariat curled in one corner of the wagon. "Oh, stop it, you nitwit!" she chided herself. "Pull yourself together! You don't know that any of that's true, and besides, you've got a rodeo to win today!" With that, she put her journal away and jumped out of the wagon, determined to practice her roping even harder than before.

The rodeo started at midmorning. The day was perfect—white clouds floated high in a deep blue sky and the sunshine sparkled with a gentle warmth. A portable fence divided the arena in two, with the adult events taking place in one half and the junior events in the other. Stevie and Carole and Lisa stood by the fence watching as a four-person color guard rode out on gorgeous paint horses and paraded the American flag around the adult side of the arena. Everyone stood at attention as the Clinchport High School Band played the national anthem.

"Pretty neat, huh?" Carole's eyes glowed with pride as she held her derby over her heart.

"Always is." Stevie smiled, replacing her cowboy hat on her head after the band had finished. "Here," she said, handing Carole and Lisa two safety pins and a sheet of paper with the number 33 in big black letters. "Would you pin this on my back?"

"Sure." Carole held the paper while Lisa pinned it straight across Stevie's shoulders. "I'm glad you got thirty-three, Stevie. It feels like a real lucky number."

"Do you think so?" Stevie twisted around and tried to read her back. "Gabriel's got number seven."

"Oh, thirty-three's a whole lot luckier than seven," Lisa assured her.

"It better be," Stevie said grimly with a flinty, determined look in her eyes.

"Hey, Stevie. Relax!" Carole grinned and wiggled her red rubber nose. "This may be a competition, but don't forget it's still supposed to be fun!"

"I know." Stevie walked in a little circle and began to twirl her lariat nervously. "I just wish they would go ahead and start."

"Ladies and gentlemen," the ring announcer called a moment later. "Welcome to Clinchport's Pioneer Days Rodeo! The first events of the day will be barrel racing for the juniors and bronc riding for the adults. All riders, take your places now!"

"Good luck, Stevie!" Lisa and Carole each gave Stevie a quick hug. "We'll see you in the ring."

"Thanks!" Stevie said as she hurried off to join the other contestants. "I'll need it!"

San Antonio Sal walked out into the center of the ring and waved for Lisa and Carole to join her. As they had discussed the day before, they would clown the first event on foot, since no bucking calves or slippery goats would need to be caught.

"Are y'all feeling funny?" Sal asked as they trotted out to meet her.

"We sure are," Carole said, looking at the three barrels placed in a big triangle in the middle of the ring. It was around these barrels that Stevie would soon be racing.

"And how's our cowgirl Stevie doing?" Sal's red painted-on eyebrows wrinkled in concern.

"She's nervous," said Lisa. "But she's determined to win, and she's a pretty good barrel racer."

"Good for her." Sal grinned. "All right, Texarkana Lisa

and Texarkana Carole, if y'all are ready, then let's rock and roll!"

The girls followed Sal over to the sidelines, where they began their first routine—one where Sal and Carole fought over who got to push Lisa around in a baby carriage. Carole had just started the fight by bopping Sal over the head with a rubber bat when the ring announcer spoke.

"Our first junior barrel racer is Ms. Mary Corona from Arden Springs. Give her a big howdy, folks!"

Applause rippled through the crowd. The girls clowned through their routine while Mary Corona raced around the barrels. "If we keep an ear on the announcer, we can hear when Stevie's turn comes," Carole whispered as Lisa honked her big rubber nose.

"I know." Lisa winked back as Mary Corona crossed the finish line and the crowd laughed at their antics.

Clowning all the way, Sal and Carole pushed Lisa in the buggy down toward the middle of the arena. Over in the adult part of the rodeo, cowboys were trying to remain seated on bucking broncos while their crowd cheered. The other team of rodeo clowns and the pickup riders were working hard to see that all the cowboys got off their broncs and out of the arena safely.

"Wow," Lisa said as Sal stopped the baby carriage. "Looks like they're working a lot harder than we are."

"They are right now, but just wait till those goats come out," laughed Sal.

"Look!" Carole pointed to the far end of the arena. "Stevie's up next. I can see her at the starting line. And Gabriel's right after her!"

"Okay," Sal said. "I'll start juggling so y'all can watch, but remember not to cheer for her. We're clowns, and clowns root for everybody."

Sal started juggling three bowling pins while Carole and Lisa pretended to fight over the baby carriage. "Our next contestant is Ms. Stevie Lake," the announcer said. "All the way from Willow Creek, Virginia! Let's give this little Southern belle a big hand!"

The crowd cheered. All the pioneers from the wagon train were sitting together, so an especially loud chorus of whistles and cheers went up from them. Carole and Lisa looked at each other and rolled their eyes at the idea of Stevie's being a Southern belle. Then the starting buzzer sounded. They paused in their make-believe fight and held their breath as Stevie and Tumbleweed shot out of the chute. Stevie leaned into the first turn just as Jeannie and Eli had taught her at the Bar None Ranch; then they flew toward the second barrel. Tumbleweed's ears were slapped back as he galloped, and the girls could see a look of grim determination on Stevie's face. They twisted around the last barrel, then dashed toward the finish line. As they crossed it, a huge cheer went up from the crowd. Carole could see Mr. Cate standing up and whistling while Karen Nicely rang a cowbell.

"Whoa, Nellie!" the ring announcer cried. "That little

Southern belle can ride!" He paused, then continued, "Our next contestant is Gabriel Jackson, who's visiting us from Montana. Let her rip, Gabriel!"

Lisa and Carole watched as Gabriel and Napoleon took their place behind the starting line. When the buzzer sounded, the big palomino burst forward in a rush. He and Gabriel slid around the first barrel and raced to the second. They circled it cleanly. Gabriel leaned forward in the saddle and whacked Napoleon's rump as they circled the last barrel and rode hard toward the finish line. Again a cheer arose from the crowd as Gabriel pulled up in a cloud of dust.

"Nice job, young man," the ring announcer said. "That's all our barrel racing contestants, folks, and in just a moment we'll announce our results."

"What do you think?" Lisa asked Carole nervously.

"I don't know." Carole frowned. "They both looked awfully fast from this end of the arena."

They hurried back to where Sal was trying to juggle a tennis racket, a baseball bat, and a feather. The crowd roared with laughter as she got two things going but never all three together.

"How'd she do?" Sal whispered as the tennis racket came crashing to the ground at her feet.

"We don't know yet," said Carole. "They're figuring up the results."

"Well, we need to go get on our horses," Sal said. "Lisa, hop back in the baby carriage and we'll exit stage left."

Lisa sprawled comically in the buggy just as the ring announcer's voice rang out. "Ladies and gentlemen, today's champion junior barrel racer is our little Southern belle, Ms. Stevie Lake from Willow Creek, Virginia!"

Lisa started to clap but caught herself. "One down," she whispered happily to Carole as they rolled toward the exit. "Four to go!"

The next event was goat wrestling. It worked much like bulldogging, with the riders tackling goats, instead of calves, from horseback and pinning them to the ground. Though goats weighed less than calves, they were faster and a lot nimbler. Sal reminded the girls what their jobs were as they hurried over to their horses.

"Now, remember. Carole will act just like a hazer in calf roping and make sure the goat keeps running straight. Lisa, you'll make sure the rider's okay at all times, and I'll worry about making everything seem funny for the crowd."

"Where do we herd the goats after they've been pinned?" Carole asked as she made sure Pogo's cinch was tight.

Sal mounted Sadie and peered into the arena. "Head 'em over to that stock pen by the speaker's stand. The pickup boys want to save that big pen beside the racetrack for some of the nastier bulls the adults will ride."

"Okay," the girls said as they mounted up. They rode to the gate and waited as the grounds crew removed the barrels and set up the goat chute. Then they loped out onto the field, doing Sal's famous chase routine. By the time they had the crowd howling with laughter, the goat wrestling was ready to begin. Carole took her place on one side of the goat chute while Lisa rode over next to the riders' gate. Sal trotted down to the far end of the arena and began pulling balloons out of Sadie's left ear.

The first contestant was Mary Corona, the girl who had competed in barrel racing. She settled her horse down inside the gate, then gave a quick nod. The chute opened and a big white billy goat came charging out. Carole urged Pogo into a lope to keep up with him while Mary Corona burst out of her gate on a beautiful pinto mare. Lisa and Ghost followed slightly behind Mary as she chased the goat down one side of the arena. Mary leaned low over the goat's body, then grabbed his neck and slid off her horse. Though she pulled backward with all her strength, the goat managed to wiggle away from her. She chased him for a few steps, then lunged at his hind leg. He gave a small kick, then scurried away again as Mary Corona fell facedown in the dust. The buzzer sounded.

"Sorry, Mary, your time is up," the rodeo announcer said. "But give her a nice hand, anyway, folks. That was a good try."

Carole and Pogo herded the bleating goat over to the stock pen while Lisa reached down from Ghost and offered Mary a hand.

"Are you okay?" she asked.

"Yeah, I'm fine," the girl replied, dusting off her lacy

71

white cowboy shirt. "Just disappointed. This goat stuff is harder than it looks."

"Well, good luck in the next event," Lisa called as Mary walked back to the starting gate.

Carole returned, and they took their places again. The next three contestants had no luck at all. Carole and Lisa were beginning to wonder if anybody could successfully wrestle a goat when Gabriel's name was announced.

"Here's our young cowpoke from Montana again," the announcer said as Gabriel rode Napoleon into the starting gate. Carole and Lisa watched for the nod of his black cowboy hat. Then the chutes opened and his goat was off and running. Almost before Carole and Lisa could blink, Gabriel was off Napoleon and had the goat on his back, three of his legs tied with a bow. The crowd cheered.

"What a ride!" the announcer cried. "Tip your hat to the audience, young man! You're one heck of a goat-buster!"

Smiling, Gabriel took off his hat and waved to the audience. The girls watched as he remounted Napoleon and rode triumphantly around the ring.

"Watch out," Lisa whispered to Carole as they got back into position. "I think Stevie's next!"

"Our last contestant is Ms. Stevie Lake, from Virginia," the announcer said. "If she can wrestle a goat as well as she can circle a barrel, then all us Western cowboys are in trouble!"

Stevie and Tumbleweed settled down into the starting gate. Carole and Lisa both had butterflies in their stomachs as they watched a wrangler push a big black-and-white goat into the chute. They waited for Stevie's signal. The gates flew open.

The goat came out fast, but Tumbleweed was just as fast, running right alongside him. Stevie waited for an instant, choosing just the right moment, then leaned low over the goat and slid off Tumbleweed. She grabbed the goat by his neck and front leg, but she misjudged how fast he was running. Instead of pulling him down, Stevie rolled head over heels and pulled the goat upside down on top of her! Carole and Lisa could only watch helplessly while his four legs and Stevie's two legs flailed in the air. The audience roared with laughter, but Stevie and the goat kept scrambling around in the dirt. She'd finally managed to climb to her feet and grab his stubby little tail when the buzzer sounded. Her time had run out. She let go of the goat and watched as he scampered away to the other side of the ring.

"Nice try, Stevie!" the announcer laughed. "You just gave a whole new meaning to the term *goat wrestling*. Give her a big hand, folks!"

The crowd applauded. "Stevie, are you okay?" Lisa asked worriedly. The goat had mashed Stevie's hat flat, and Stevie wore a thin layer of brown dust from head to toe.

"Yes, I'm fine," she said, rubbing her elbow. "But that sure didn't feel like any normal goat. They must have fed him Mexican jumping beans or something."

"Well, wave to the crowd so they'll know you're all right. Mr. Cate and Polly Shaver and Karen Nicely are all up there cheering for you," Lisa said. "And don't worry about it. The audience loves you, and you've still got three events to go!"

"You're right." Stevie grinned and pushed her hat back into shape. She waved to the crowd, and everyone cheered even more loudly. *Three events to go,* she thought as she walked back to the gates. *And I've got to win at least two of them!*

THE NEXT EVENT was calf roping. Since the grounds crew didn't need to set anything up, Lisa and Carole and Sal stayed on their horses and waited for the action to begin. Carole was to haze the calves just as she had done with the goats, and Lisa was to keep an eye on the riders. Sal clowned and coordinated them from the far end of the ring.

As before, Mary Corona was the first contestant. She bounded out on her pinto mare and roped her calf successfully, but the calf had long, wiggly legs and she lost a lot of time trying to tie them up. The next few contestants did better. Then it was Gabriel's turn. He carefully positioned Napoleon in the gate, then nodded. With the same lightning speed he'd used in the goat wrestling, he roped his calf and had its legs tied almost before Carole and Lisa could blink. They had nothing to do but sit on their horses and watch while he took his hat off and waved again to the cheering crowd.

"Give that young man a hand," the announcer cried as Gabriel and Napoleon made another triumphant circle around the ring. "He's as fast a calf roper as he is a goat wrestler!"

Stevie was next. Carole and Lisa glanced worriedly at each other as she got ready to ride. When she settled down in the gate they turned their attention to the business at hand. With a quick nod, Stevie signaled to open the chute. She and Tumbleweed thundered out of the gate just behind a brown calf that galloped along like a little racehorse. The calf tried to veer off to the right, but Carole rode alongside him and kept him running straight. Stevie began swinging her lasso in a tight circle, and when Tumbleweed had drawn even with the calf's shoulders, she let the noose go. It fell over his head, right on target. Immediately Tumbleweed stopped and began to back up, keeping the rope taut. Stevie leaped off the right side of the saddle and rushed down to the calf. She had no difficulty pulling him over, but his legs flailed as wildly as the goat's, and it took her a long time to tie three of them together. When she finally stood up and held her arms out, her time had almost run out. She looked disappointedly at Lisa and Carole as she got back on Tumbleweed, and when they announced the winners of the event, Gabriel had come in first, Stevie a distant third.

"Uh-oh," Lisa said to Carole after the announcer had read the results. "It's two events to one, in favor of Gabriel. I think Stevie might really be in trouble."

"I know." Carole frowned. "I hate to admit this, but Gabriel is really good. If Stevie doesn't win the pole bending and the quarter-mile race, she's going to be doing something awful."

"Wonder what it will be?" asked Lisa.

"I don't even want to think about it," said Carole with a grimace.

They trotted down to the end of the ring, where Sal was pretending for the crowd that she and Sadie had both fallen asleep. After she ended her bit to a round of applause, she rode over to Carole and Lisa.

"Let's give the horses a rest while they set up for the pole bending," Sal suggested. She removed her oversized polka-dot nightcap and smiled. "Y'all have clowned hard and you've done a terrific job. Why don't you go take a break as well? They won't need us again until after the pole bending. Then we'll do the fake roundup routine, and then it'll be time for the race."

Actually, a rest didn't sound too bad to Carole and Lisa. They had ridden every turn with all the goat-wrestling and calf-roping contestants, plus they had clowned through the barrel race on foot. They dismounted and led Pogo and Ghost over to a water trough, then gave them an armful of hay in a temporary corral. The two girls sat on the fence and ate an apple while the horses munched their hay.

"Look," said Lisa, pointing toward the Rocking S stable. "Here comes Pete."

Carole looked over her shoulder. Pete was crossing the racetrack and heading straight toward them.

"Howdy, girls," he said, tipping his hat. "I saw you two over here and just wondered how everything was going. Are Ghost and Pogo behaving themselves?"

"Oh, yes, Pete, they're terrific," said Carole with a smile. It was true. Whatever the girls had asked them to do, the two quarter horses had done willingly.

Pete watched the grounds crew setting up the poles for the next event. "How's Stevie doing?"

"Well, she won the barrel race," Lisa reported proudly.

"And she came in third in the calf roping," added Carole.

"Then there was the goat wrestling." Lisa shook her head. "Don't ask. You don't even want to know about the goat wrestling."

Pete chuckled. "Those little goats can be right ornery critters." He pushed his hat back on his head. "How's her bet with her boyfriend coming along?"

"Oh, he's not her boyfriend," Lisa explained quickly. "But so far he's ahead two to one. They've got pole bending and the quarter-mile race to go."

"Well, if she remembers what I told her about Tumbleweed, she'll do fine," said Pete.

Carole frowned. "What did you tell her?"

"That all she's got to do is touch him with her spurs." Pete chuckled again. "If she does that, he'll outrun every horse in this rodeo."

"I can't imagine that Stevie would forget an important thing like that," Carole said.

"Probably not." He smiled. "Well, you tell her I came by and wished her good luck." He tipped his hat again.

"Thanks, Pete. We will." They watched him as he strolled back to the stable.

"I wonder if Stevie does remember about Tumbleweed and spurs." Carole looked at Lisa. "She's never mentioned it."

"I'm sure she does," Lisa replied. "Stevie's so focused on this rodeo she probably remembers every word that came out of Pete's mouth."

"I guess you're right," agreed Carole. "Let's ride over to the fence. I think the bull riding's about to start."

They remounted Pogo and Ghost and rode over behind the big refreshment trailer to look into the adult arena. The adult rodeo clowns were jumping around in the middle of the ring, loosening up to get ready for the bulls.

"Oh, good!" Carole stood up in her stirrups. "We can watch this until the pole bending begins. It really looks exciting!"

The first cowboy was easing himself down on the back

of a brown-and-white bull when Lisa felt someone tapping her leg. She looked down. Eileen was grinning up at her, munching on popcorn.

"You guys are doing a pretty good job of clowning," she said sweetly. "Mr. Cate and Ms. Nicely think you're really funny."

Lisa blinked in surprise. A compliment? From little Eileen? "Thanks, Eileen," she replied. "I'm glad you think so."

"Yeah," Eileen continued. "But the funniest part was when Stevie wrestled that goat and got all dirty. She looked so mad! That's been the best thing about the rodeo so far!"

"Thanks, Eileen," Carole answered sarcastically. "I know Stevie will be glad to hear how much you enjoyed that."

Eileen rattled her popcorn bag. "I know something else that Stevie would enjoy."

"What?" Lisa asked with a frown.

"She would really enjoy knowing my secret." Eileen tossed a piece of popcorn in her mouth and looked up at the girls with an overly sweet smile. "Are you sure you wouldn't like to know, too?"

Lisa and Carole looked at each other and shook their heads. "No thanks, Eileen," Lisa replied. "I don't think we need to know anything you might want to tell us."

"No, really. It's a neat thing." Eileen's green eyes

flashed. She chewed her popcorn quickly. "I mean, it's a really *important* thing! It could mean a lot to Stevie."

"Well, if it's that important, why don't you go tell Stevie yourself?" Carole asked.

Eileen pulled on Lisa's big Western stirrup. "Because she was mean to me this morning," she whined, her lower lip stuck out. "She said she was going to rope me and tie me up and make Yankee and Doodle drag me behind the wagon."

"Oh, for Pete's sake, Eileen." Lisa shook her head in disgust. "She was only kidding." She'd started to say something else when a deafening roar went up from the adult side of the arena. A huge buckskin bull with long, pointed horns had just tossed his rider high in the air. The cowboy was scrambling in the dirt, trying to avoid being gored as the bull came charging after him, his horns low and his eyes wild. All the adult clowns were waving their arms and running in circles, desperately trying to distract the angry animal from the fallen cowboy. Every time one of them went near, though, the bull shook his horns and bellowed even more loudly.

"Hold on, boys, I'm coming!" a voice called. Carole and Lisa looked over at their side of the arena. San Antonio Sal had dropped the bouquet of plastic flowers she was clowning with and was running over to help.

"Should we go, too?" Lisa asked as they watched her scramble over the fence.

"You two stay right there!" Sal called over to them. "Don't you come near this bull!"

Pulling a huge red scarf from her pocket, she ran full speed toward the snorting bull. The bright, shiny fabric must have caught his eye, because he looked up from the cowboy he was trying to gore and started to run straight at Sal. While another clown helped the shaken cowboy to his feet, Sal flapped her scarf at the bull and lured him toward the barrel, where the barrel man was poking his head up and yelling something at the bull in Spanish. Confused, the angry animal stopped and pawed the ground for a moment, his breath coming in loud snorts. As he tried to decide what to do next, the point clown sneaked along the fence and opened the temporary pen next to the racetrack.

"See if you can get him in here, Sal," the clown called. "I'll head him off this way."

Sal nodded but didn't take her eyes off the bull. "Come on, Bossy," she called to the animal sweetly. "You've already dumped your rider. Now you need to go bye-bye!"

The bull stared at her. She waved her scarf as if she were bidding someone farewell, then twirled it over her head like a lasso. The bull snorted once and ran straight at her, his hooves thundering in the dirt.

"Heads up, everybody!" the barrel man yelled. "Here he comes!"

Still twirling the scarf, Sal ran straight for the open pen. The bull chased her at a hard gallop. As fast as Sal was running, the bull was gaining on her. His horns were not ten feet away from her when she scurried into the pen and scrambled up the fence on the other side. Bellowing loudly, the bull rushed in behind her, and the point clown slammed the pen shut behind him. The stadium erupted in wild cheers.

"Folks, that was San Antonio Sal doing that fancy piece of footwork with that bull," the adult ring announcer said. "Let's give her and all our hardworking rodeo clowns a big hand!"

Sal bounded happily back into the ring and bowed, then ran over and pretended to give the limping cowboy a big kiss. The crowd roared and clapped even harder as she clowned her way back to the junior ring.

"Wow," Carole breathed as Sal climbed back over the fence. "That was really scary!"

"I know," Lisa said shakily. "My heart's beating like crazy. And look. That bull still hasn't calmed down."

Carole looked over at the temporary pen. The bull stood in the middle of it, staring at Sal, still pawing at the ground and bellowing.

"Whew!" Sal said, wiping her forehead as she walked over to the girls. "That was a close one! I didn't think that little ol' temporary fence was going to hold me when I started climbing it! It must be made out of chicken wire!"

"Sal, we were so scared," Lisa said. "I had no idea bulls were that fast."

"They can be when they're mad. Apparently that critter is having a bad rodeo day!" Sal laughed as she caught her breath. "How's the pole bending going?"

Lisa and Carole looked at each other. In all the excitement, they'd totally forgotten about the pole bending contest. Immediately they turned their attention to the junior ring, where Gabriel had just finished.

"Oh, good," Lisa said as the announcer called Stevie's name. "We haven't missed Stevie. I hope she remembers everything Sal taught her about pole bending."

"I do, too," said Carole. "That way she might at least do better at this than she did at goat wrestling. Stevie doesn't need to be the comic relief again!"

The girls watched as Stevie and Tumbleweed positioned themselves behind the starting line. The buzzer sounded, and Tumbleweed leaped forward at a gallop. They twisted around the first pole, then the second. Tumbleweed wove around the poles surefootedly, using all his quarter horse instincts. Carole and Lisa noticed that Stevie leaned back ever so slightly in the saddle when Tumbleweed changed his leads, just the way Sal had told her. They turned around the end pole in a cloud of dust, then began twisting back through the course to the finish line. Stevie's hat flew off her head again as Tumbleweed lengthened his stride into a hard gallop. A cheer went up from the crowd as they finished.

"A mighty fine run for Ms. Stevie Lake!" the announcer called. "Give her a big hand, and we'll have our winners in just a minute."

The crowd clapped for Stevie. Several wild cheers rang out from the wagon train contingent. Lisa and Carole looked at each other, wondering if Stevie had been fast enough to beat Gabriel. If Stevie didn't win this event, there would be no way she could win the rodeo, and her bet with Gabriel would be over.

"Oh, please," Lisa whispered, closing her eyes and crossing her fingers. "Let her win this one!"

Suddenly the ring announcer's voice broke the expectant stillness of the arena. "Ladies and gentlemen," he began. "I'm pleased to announce that this year's pole bending champ is none other than Ms. Stevie Lake from Willow Creek, Virginia!"

Though Carole and Lisa knew they weren't supposed to cheer, they leaned over from their horses and gave each other a hug. Again they could hear Mr. Cate's shrill whistle ringing out over Karen Nicely's wildly clanging cowbell.

"Now they're tied," said Carole. "Whoever wins the quarter-mile race will win it all!"

9

"GOOD BOY, TUMBLEWEED!" Stevie said to the sweaty quarter horse as she led him to the trough for a long drink of water. From the arena she could hear the rodeo crowd laughing at one of Sal and Lisa and Carole's routines, while just ahead of her a tractor smoothed the surface of the track in preparation for the quarter-mile race. There was a fifteen-minute break, during which the clowns would entertain the crowd and then help them relocate around the track. The break also served as a rest period for the horses and riders who'd competed in the previous events.

"You've been such a good horse!" Stevie reached over and patted Tumbleweed's lathered shoulder as he slurped long swallows of water. "Everything that's gone wrong has been my fault."

Stevie knew very well that the day's mistakes had, indeed, been hers. Tumbleweed had performed perfectly, from racing after the goat at just the right speed to holding the calf tightly on the line while Stevie tried to tie his feet. "I guess I'm just not too hot with four-legged nonhorse creatures," she said with a shrug.

She looked at Tumbleweed. "But I'm real good when it's just me alone, and we're great together!" She grinned as Tumbleweed raised his head from the water trough, his chin dripping. "Now we've just got one more event to go. If we can win this race, it won't matter how badly I wrestle goats or rope calves!"

She led Tumbleweed to the concession trailer and leaned against him as Carole and Lisa chased Sal around the arena, trying to rope her with string they squirted out of a can. She smiled as she watched her friends clowning for the crowd and making everyone laugh. "I bet Phil's not doing anything like that right now," she whispered. "I bet he's probably paddling down some river with Meghan or Chelsea or whatever her name is. She's wearing some really cute outfit, and they're probably planning their next vacation together, which will be something really glamorous and exciting, like climbing the Himalayas." Just at that moment Tumbleweed shifted on his feet and gave a big sigh. "I know exactly how you feel, boy," Stevie said sadly as she rubbed the horse behind his ears.

"Hi, Stevie."

Stevie looked up to see Eileen, dressed in her pioneer clothes and holding a cone of pink cotton candy.

"Hi, Eileen," she replied.

"I saw you try to wrestle that little goat. You were pretty funny. Everybody laughed at you."

"Oh, really?" Stevie's cheeks started to burn—not at the thought of the crowd laughing at her, but at the thought of Mr. Hotshot Rodeo Star Gabriel laughing at her.

"Yes, it was *really* funny." Eileen bit into her cotton candy. "I laughed the hardest."

"I bet you did, Eileen." Stevie took off her cowboy hat and wiped the sweat from her forehead.

"You know, I still know that secret," Eileen began again.

"What secret?"

"The one I tried to tell you this morning."

Stevie frowned. "You mean when you came over to the wagon and bugged us while we were trying to get ready?"

Eileen nodded.

"I thought you were making up that secret business just to be a pest."

"No," said Eileen. "I really do have a secret."

"Sorry, Eileen." Stevie turned back toward Tumbleweed. "I don't think you could possibly know anything that I would be the least bit interested in learning."

"You never know," Eileen taunted her. "I mean, I

might know something that you might need to know, because if you didn't, something terrible might happen."

"Go watch the rodeo, Eileen," Stevie said as she checked Tumbleweed's right front shoe. "Go see what the clowns are doing."

"And then if something terrible happened and you didn't know because you hadn't bothered to ask . . ."

"Eileen, I—"

"And then you'd really feel horrible if—"

"All right!" Stevie said so sharply that Tumbleweed jumped. "I give up! Eileen, whatever this vitally important secret is, please, just go ahead and spit it out now!"

Eileen started to poke out her lower lip in her usual pout but then changed her mind. "Okay." She took a step toward Stevie and spoke just above a whisper. "This is what I overheard Gabriel telling Shelly Bean at lunch the other day. He told Shelly that you two had a bet, and whoever won the most rodeo events would get to make the other perform a secret dare."

Stevie rolled her eyes and slapped her hat back on her head. "Sorry, Eileen, but that's old news. I was there when we made the bet. I already know all that stuff."

"But wait. There's more. I heard what Gabriel's secret dare is!" Eileen's green eyes glittered.

Stevie looked at Eileen and frowned. As much as she disliked the idea of getting any information at all from this bratty little girl, Gabriel's secret dare was something worth knowing. "What?" she finally asked reluctantly.

Eileen grinned. "Gabriel's going to dare you to be his date for the big barbecue dinner tonight, and he wants to make you rush up and give him a big kiss when he accepts his first-prize award!"

"What?" Stevie was stunned. She grew first hot, then cold, and her head spun. This was far worse than anything she had ever imagined! She had thought she would just make Gabriel put on her pioneer dress and milk Veronica. She figured he would make her do something like saying over and over that he was the best rodeo rider in the world while she cleaned out Napoleon's stall. She had no idea Gabriel would want to make her kiss him! And worse, in front of everybody!

No way! She turned and furiously checked all the buckles on Tumbleweed's tack. Nohow! She smoothed Tumbleweed's saddle blanket and gave him a brisk pat on his rump. They were going to win this race. Even if she had to carry Tumbleweed across the finish line on her back, she would do it to avoid having to kiss Gabriel!

"All quarter-mile racers, please report to the track," said the ring announcer's voice.

Stevie hopped up on Tumbleweed. She looked down at Eileen, whose mouth was now ringed with pink cotton-candy stains. "Thanks, Eileen. You've just let me know how much is at stake in this race."

"So it was a pretty good secret, huh?" Eileen asked proudly.

"Eileen, it was one of the best I've heard in a long time. Now go find your parents and watch me beat Gabriel."

"Oh, goody!" Eileen said as she scurried off to the grandstand.

Stevie and Tumbleweed trotted over to the starting line, steering clear of the angry bull, which was still snorting at everyone who came near his pen. Stevie saw that Carole and Lisa and Sal were clowning on horseback, leading the crowd from the arena stands and out toward the track so that they could watch the race more closely. Lisa and Sal had exited the grandstand at the far end of the arena while Carole had ridden out closer to Stevie. She and Pogo stood between the starting line and the pen that held the cantankerous bull. Stevie waved at Carole, who waved back and then started making kicking motions with her feet. Stevie frowned and looked down at her boots. What was Carole trying to tell her? Had she stepped on a candy wrapper or something?

"Riders, take your places behind the starting line, please!" A man wearing a black ten-gallon hat was speaking through a bullhorn. Stevie forgot about her boots and trotted Tumbleweed up to a tape that stretched across the track. Mary Corona, riding her pinto, was already there, as were some riders Stevie didn't recognize. She was just beginning to wonder where Gabriel was when she heard a familiar voice behind her.

"Hey, Miss I Can Pin a Goat to the Ground in Eight

Seconds! How's it going?" Gabriel laughed and pulled Napoleon up right beside her. Stevie had never realized how much bigger Napoleon was than Tumbleweed, and how his coat seemed to glitter like gold in the sun. Gabriel reined him back a little. "I had no idea you were going to go for laughs in the goat wrestling. I thought your friends were supposed to be the clowns today!"

"They needed some help in that event, Mr. Can't Bend a Pole or Race a Barrel Too Fast," Stevie snapped back. "The crowd was getting bored with a certain contestant taking all these grand tours of the arena, waving to them on his golden palomino!"

"They seemed to like it," Gabriel replied. "Although I have to admit, it wasn't as funny as watching you and that goat flop around in the dust!" He laughed again and eyed Stevie's filthy cowboy shirt. "Too bad about your nice clean shirt."

"Too bad about yours, too," she said sadly.

"Mine?" Gabriel frowned and looked down at his almost spotless white shirt.

"Yeah." Stevie grinned. "In about two minutes it's going to be covered in my dust when this race begins. By the time we cross the finish line, you'll be able to write your initials across it!"

"Oh, right," Gabriel snorted. "In your dreams." He pulled his hat down over his eyes and gave Napoleon's golden shoulder a pat.

"More like in my nightmares if you've got anything to

do with them," Stevie snapped back, getting mad all over again at the idea of him making her kiss him.

"Riders, get ready to go!" the man with the bullhorn announced. "Halfway around the track is a quarter mile." He lifted the starting gun.

Suddenly the riders grew silent and concentrated on the stretch of track ahead of them. Even the horses quivered with anticipation, eager to burst down the track as fast as they could go. Farther away, by the first turn, Stevie could see Sal and Lisa sitting on their horses, looking toward them, waiting for the race to begin. How proud they would be when she won! She leaned low and forward in the saddle and grasped the reins tightly, waiting for the blast of the starting gun. She had turned her head one last time to shoot a menacing scowl at Gabriel when suddenly an odd movement caught her eye. Just behind Carole and Pogo, the angry bull was hooking the flimsy fence with his horns. The fence wobbled, then sagged to the ground. The bull was free! He leaped forward and pawed the ground once as he sniffed the air, then lowered his head and began to charge. And he began to charge straight at Carole and Pogo!

THE CRACK OF the starting gun split the air. All the other horses sprang forward. Tumbleweed's first impulse was to do the same, but Stevie reined him hard to the left. Immediately he obeyed, pivoting with his quarter horse agility.

"Come on, Tumbleweed!" She squeezed with her legs and urged him forward, faster than she'd ever wanted him to go before, but he seemed stuck in his regular lope. Though it was fast, it wasn't nearly fast enough to get to Carole in time.

"Come on, Tumbleweed," she said again. She leaned closer to him and squeezed him again, but it did no good. It was as if he were stuck going fifty miles an hour when he could easily have gone eighty. Then Stevie remembered something Pete had told her. "Don't use your spurs on

94

Tumbleweed unless you want him to take off like a rocket."
Your spurs! That was what Carole had been trying to signal
her right before the race! Instantly Stevie jammed her
heels into Tumbleweed's side. He hesitated for an instant,
then leaped across the track faster than he'd ever gone
before. His flying mane whipped Stevie's face, but she
maintained her race position—low and forward in the saddle. Some of the spectators, astonished by her actions, were
just beginning to realize what was happening. Several people had seen the bull and began running away from the
track, their children clutched in their arms.

From the corner of her eye, Stevie could see that Lisa
and Sal had also spotted the trouble Carole was in and
had begun to race toward her. The other rodeo clowns
were scrambling from the adult arena to help, and the
pickup cowboys were galloping to the exit at the end of
the arena. Still, Stevie was closest to the bull. She was the
only one who could reach Carole in time.

Tumbleweed was now halfway across the track. Though
Carole and Pogo were trying to side-pass around the bull,
he had them trapped in the corner between the grandstand and the back of the concession trailer. They had no
room to maneuver, and his deadly horns were getting
closer and closer. Carole kept Pogo moving from side to
side, but Stevie could already see the whites showing
around Pogo's terrified eyes. If Pogo grew any more fright-
ened, she could panic and buck Carole off, leaving her
totally defenseless in front of the bull.

95

Frantically, Stevie racked her brain. Why hadn't she listened when Carole and Lisa had talked about clowning? What had they said clowns did when bulls went crazy? Banged on a barrel or something like that. But Stevie had no barrel to bang on. All she had was Tumbleweed and herself. "Think!" she whispered as they thundered closer to the bull. "Think!"

Stevie was almost there. She could see white foam curling from Pogo's mouth. She jammed her heels into Tumbleweed's side again. He bore down and went even faster. "Hey!" Stevie screamed at the bull at the top of her lungs. "Hey! Bossy! Over here!"

The bull paid no attention. He kept moving closer and closer to Carole, now snorting, now shaking his horns from side to side. "Hey!" Stevie yelled again. Then she spied Sal's big red scarf lying on the ground. Sal must have dropped it after she'd lured the bull into the pen the first time around. If that scarf had worked with this bull once, maybe it would work again.

Stevie shifted her weight slightly to the left and leaned low in the saddle, using the same motions she'd used when she was trying to slide off Tumbleweed on top of the goat. Instinctively Tumbleweed veered slightly to the left, carrying Stevie closer to the scarf. In all her life she'd never leaned so low to the ground on horseback before, but with one swooping motion, clinging to the saddle horn, she stretched her left arm out as far as it would go. Her fingertips grazed the silky red material. She stretched to her absolute limit and tried to grab it. She got it! She clutched it in her hand as she pulled herself back into the saddle and urged Tumbleweed forward again. She wondered for a moment whether Tumbleweed would sense Pogo's fear and balk at running so close to the bull. Most horses would flee from an animal that was snorting and bellowing in rage. But the little quarter horse didn't flinch. He galloped on, obeying her commands without question.

Stevie pointed him straight at the bull's side, then reined him up about ten feet away. "Hey, Ferdinand!" Stevie yelled at the bull. "Look at this!" She flapped the red scarf. The bull saw it out of the corner of his eye and turned to look. For a moment his vicious horns pointed away from Carole and Pogo.

"Hey, Ferdinand!" Stevie called again. *"Toro, toro, toro!"* She loosened her grip on Tumbleweed's reins and held the scarf out beside her the way a bullfighter would hold a cape. Jiggling one end of the scarf, she waved it back and forth in front of the bull. He looked at it for a moment, then turned the rest of his huge body to face it. That gave Carole and Pogo enough room to leap out of the corner where they'd been trapped. Carole stopped Pogo just beyond the reach of the bull's horns, then began to wave her derby at him from the other direction.

For a few more seconds the girls worked hard to keep the bull flustered. The bull didn't know which one to try to gore first, so he just stood there, shaking his horns at both of them and pawing the ground. After what seemed like hours, the adult team of rodeo clowns made it through the grandstand. They jumped around and further confused the bull, then joined hands and made a shield in front of Stevie and Carole while the two cowboys arrived and threw lassos around the bull's neck. Finally realizing he was outnumbered and roped, the bull gave one last bellow and allowed the cowboys to lead him back to the main stock trailer.

"Are you girls okay?" one of the clowns asked after the bull had been led away.

"I think so." Stevie looked at Carole and Pogo. They both seemed shaken.

"Maybe you two should go and take it easy for a little while," the clown suggested. "Petunia can be a handful when he gets riled up, but you two did a great job containing him."

Stevie frowned. "That bull's name is Petunia?"

The clown shrugged. "So go figure. I guess whoever named him didn't know too much about cattle."

"Whatever." Stevie chuckled with relief. She handed Sal's red scarf to the clown and trotted over to Carole. "Are you okay?"

"I think so," said Carole. "But let's go somewhere else. Pogo and I need to get as far away from Petunia as we possibly can."

The two girls rode over to Lisa and Sal. Though it

seemed to Stevie that the whole incident had taken hours, in reality it had ended in less than a minute. Lisa and Sal had galloped at full speed from the other end of the track, and they were just now arriving.

"Stevie! Carole! Are you two all right?" Lisa looked sickly pale. Her eyes were wide with fear.

"We're okay," said Stevie, although her mouth was dry and her heart was thumping like a drum.

"You two sure did a great job of bull wrangling!" Sal said, beaming at them.

"Thanks," Carole said. "Now I think I'd like to sit down a minute."

Everyone dismounted, giving the horses a well-deserved rest. Carole soothed the still-trembling Pogo while Stevie rubbed Tumbleweed affectionately behind his ears. He had done a wonderfully brave job.

"I was so scared," Lisa said, her voice shaking. "Sal and I came as soon as we saw what was happening." She looked at Carole and Stevie with tears in her eyes. "That bull had you trapped! Both of you and the horses could have been killed!"

"I suppose." Stevie took her cowboy hat off. "It's funny, but that didn't occur to me until the clowns led that bull away."

"Me neither," added Carole. She grinned at Stevie. "I kept wondering what you were going to do if he decided to charge that scarf!"

Stevie laughed. "I hadn't figured that out yet." She

looked at Carole quizzically. "Hey, were you trying to tell me to use my heels on Tumbleweed right before the race?"

Carole nodded. "Pete came by to wish you luck and hoped you'd remember what he'd told you about Tumbleweed and spurs."

"I couldn't figure out what you meant until we were halfway across the track," Stevie said. "But I'm glad I remembered it when I did!"

"I'm glad you did, too!" Lisa shook her head. "You two nearly gave me a heart attack!"

"Then let's have a group hug and be grateful we've got lucky stars," suggested Stevie, holding her arms open wide.

The three girls clutched each other, happy that they were all alive and unhurt. Sal joined in, grabbing a handful of tiny silver stars from one of her deep clown pockets and sprinkling them over the girls. They had just begun to laugh about how funny Stevie looked with stars in her damp, tousled hair when Gabriel rode up on Napoleon.

"Hi," he said, reining the big palomino in close. He hopped off and pulled the reins over Napoleon's head. "I just heard what happened with the bull. Are you okay, Carole?"

"Yes, I am, thanks to Stevie." Carole smiled.

"And are you okay?" Gabriel turned to Stevie and for once looked at her without a teasing expression.

"I'm fine, thanks," she replied. Suddenly she remembered that this whole thing had started right as she was beginning the quarter-mile race—the event that would decide who won their bet. "Hey," she said. "Who won the race? I kind of got distracted and forgot all about it."

"Oh, haven't you heard?" Gabriel asked, his old teasing grin returning. "Me, of course. I beat Mary Corona by half a length." He stuck his thumbs in the belt loops of his jeans. "Which means that I won three out of the five events. Which means that I also won the rodeo and our bet!"

Stevie stood still. Her face grew hot with embarrassment at having been beaten, but then she smiled. She had lost the rodeo fair and square, but she had lost it for a good reason—helping to save her friend. There was nothing to be ashamed of about that.

"You're absolutely right," she told Gabriel graciously. "Congratulations!"

She held out her hand. Gabriel took it and they shook.

"Now," Stevie said. "What is it that you want me to do?"

"Oh, how about I tell you later?" he replied with another impish grin, his blue eyes looking bluer than ever.

"Okay." Stevie gulped, her palms growing sweaty. "When?"

"How about tonight? Just before the big barbecue dinner?"

"That's fine." Stevie tried to smile through the butterflies that were beginning to flit in her stomach. "I can hardly wait to hear what you've dreamed up."

"Stevie, what a wonderful rescue you accomplished today!" Mr. Cate stopped behind Stevie's chair, put one arm around her shoulders, and gave her a squeeze. He looked over at Gabriel, who was sitting beside her, beaming proudly. "You did a great rodeo job, too, young man," Mr. Cate added with a grin. Then he noticed the two empty plates on the table in front of them.

"You guys know you can get seconds on the barbecue, don't you?" Mr. Cate clutched his own second helping in his free hand, balancing a large plate piled high with barbecued ribs, corn bread, and a thick slice of apple pie.

Stevie smiled at her old friend from the wagon train. "Thanks, Mr. Cate. I think I may go get some more pie. It's really delicious!"

"Would you like me to go with you?" Gabriel asked, rising from his chair. "Or I could bring you a piece."

"No, thanks," said Stevie. "I can do it by myself."

She walked to the back of the room, where a large buffet table was covered with huge platters of food. In one corner of the room, a band consisting of a guitarist, a fiddler, and an accordionist played over the happy hum of wagon train pioneers and rodeo riders laughing and talking. Stevie put a hefty slice of apple pie on her plate and walked back to her seat next to Gabriel. She shot Carole and Lisa a dirty look when they giggled as Gabriel rose and pulled Stevie's chair out for her. The next thing she knew, a camera flash popped. Polly Shaver had snapped their picture together. Stevie smiled broadly, then started in on her pie.

Gabriel watched as she ate. "You know, I really didn't mean to make fun of you quite so hard over the goat wrestling contest," he said suddenly, his voice cracking.

"That's okay." Stevie shrugged. "I guess it was pretty funny."

"And I didn't really mean it when I said the only rodeo event you'd be good at was the cow chip tossing contest," he continued.

"Don't worry about it," Stevie said through a mouthful of pie.

"And when I said that—"

"Look." Stevie swallowed and looked at him. "We both

said some really stupid things. We both got on each other's nerves. But it's okay. When you offered to call the rodeo a draw and not hold me to our bet, that made up for everything."

"Well, it seemed like the least I could do after you saved Carole from that bull," he mumbled, suddenly staring hard at his glass of iced tea.

"It's just too bad we'll never find out how bad Tumbleweed could have beaten Napoleon," Stevie said.

Gabriel turned quickly in his chair to say something back. Then he saw that she was smiling. "Okay," he laughed. "You got me on that one."

Stevie returned her attention to her pie. In a way it was a shame that she and Tumbleweed had not competed in the race. Tumbleweed was incredibly fast once you put your spurs to him, and it would have been fun to find out which horse could have won. Still, she had no regrets about what she'd done. If anything had happened to Carole or Pogo because she wanted to compete in a horse race . . . well, she didn't even want to think about that. And it had been nice of Gabriel to walk over to their wagon and offer to call it a draw. Stevie stole a glance at him out of the corner of her eye. *Thank goodness I won't have to kiss him in front of all these people*, she thought, her palms growing sweaty all over again.

"Hey, check out those two!" Carole whispered to Lisa. They were sitting a few seats down the table from Stevie and Gabriel.

"I know." Lisa glanced over at them. "For once they actually seem to be enjoying each other's company instead of boasting about who's better or faster or stronger."

Carole giggled. "Look at the way Stevie's smiling at him!"

"And look at the way he's smiling back!" Lisa winked. "I think they both have huge, world-class crushes on each other."

"I think you're right."

"And why not?" continued Lisa. "They're both neat people. We already know what a wonderful person Stevie is. And even though Gabriel can be an arrogant know-it-all, he's got some good points, too."

Carole nodded. "He's got those killer blue eyes, he knows everything about the Oregon Trail, he rides like a dream, plus he's helping us with our notes for Deborah's newspaper assignment."

Lisa smiled. "With all the information he's given us, we should have an awesome outline for Deborah by the time we get back to Willow Creek."

Just then Mr. Williams, the president of the rodeo association, stood up at the head table. "Ladies and gentlemen," he said into a large microphone. "It's now time to present the rodeo awards. Please come forward when your name is called and collect your prize."

The crowd cheered. Several cowboys gave earsplitting whistles that echoed around the room. All eyes were on Mr. Williams at the podium.

The adult prizes were given out first. One cowboy who was dressed all in black took the award for the bronc riding contest. Another came up in a fringed buckskin jacket to accept the bull riding prize. Several other awards were passed out, and then the cowboy who'd won the most points overall was called onstage. Mr. Williams shook his hand, presented him with a check for $500, and then handed him a huge gold belt buckle that had a bucking horse stamped on it. The crowd cheered while the cowboy looked at the audience with tears in his eyes.

"I know five hundred dollars is a lot of money," he said. "But I'll spend that pretty fast. This belt buckle I'll treasure the rest of my life! Thanks a lot!"

Everyone clapped as he sat down. Mr. Williams took the microphone again.

"Next we have our junior riders. This year's competition was fierce, but our overall junior rodeo champ is Gabriel Jackson from the Wagons West trail ride." Mr. Williams looked out into the audience. "Come on up here, Gabriel, and get your prize."

Polly's camera flashed again as Gabriel rose from his chair and walked to the podium. Mr. Williams shook his hand, then gave him a long blue ribbon and a gold trophy with a bronc rider on top. Gabriel grinned and looked very proud.

"Give that young cowboy a big hand, folks!" Mr. Williams said as Gabriel made his way back to the table.

Stevie looked wistfully at the shining bronc rider on the top of his trophy as he sat beside her. It would have been neat, she thought, if she could have brought a trophy home to show Max and Deborah and her family.

"Now, we have something special for you folks tonight," Mr. Williams continued. "Normally we don't do anything like this, but normally we don't have anything like this happen. There is someone very special sitting in our audience tonight who this afternoon exhibited an extraordinary amount of courage and bravery. Would Ms. Stevie Lake please come forward?"

Stevie looked questioningly at Carole and Lisa as everyone turned to smile at her. She frowned. What was all this about?

"Go, Stevie," Polly whispered from across the table. "They're waiting for you! I'll take your picture!"

Stevie rose from her chair and walked to the podium.

"Ladies and gentlemen, for the one or two of you who might not have heard, we had a dangerous and regrettable incident with one of our bulls this afternoon when he escaped a stock pen and cornered one of our clowns. Even though Stevie was already lined up for the quarter-mile race, she saw what was happening and rushed over to save her friend, Carole Hanson." Mr. Williams put his arm around Stevie's shoulders. "Stevie, we thank you for your quick thinking and your courage, and we'd like to present you with this in honor of your bravery."

Mr. Williams held out a small black box. Stevie opened

107

it. Inside was a golden belt buckle just like the one the champion cowboy had won. "Gosh," she breathed, awed by the beautiful gift. "Thanks."

"Hold it up so that everyone can see, Stevie," Mr. Williams suggested.

Stevie grinned and held the belt buckle high above her head. The whole audience stood up and cheered. Stevie could see Carole and Lisa and Mr. Cate and Polly all clapping for her. Jeremy Barksdale and Karen Nicely and even little Eileen cheered as well. Then she saw a figure climb up on a chair. It was Gabriel, clapping hardest of all.

"Hey, Stevie," he yelled above the applause. "Catch this!" He stopped clapping and with one hand blew her a big kiss. Everyone in the audience roared!

Stevie's face reddened with embarrassment. How could Gabriel do that! Everyone knew they'd practically been at each other's throats throughout the expedition, and now he was blowing her kisses. She turned away from the cheering crowd and shook Mr. Williams's hand. By the time she returned to her seat, Gabriel had gone to help the men clear away some of the tables for square dancing.

"Hey, Stevie, let's see what they gave you!" Carole and Lisa grabbed the chairs on either side of Stevie. She laid the belt buckle on the white tablecloth, where it glowed gold in the soft light. Stevie turned it over. Mr. Williams had explained that her name and the date would be engraved on the back.

108

"Wow," said Lisa. "It's just like that cowboy said. You can keep this forever."

"You sure can." Carole ran a finger over the buckle. "You can always remember that this was the day you saved my life!"

"Oh, I'll remember a lot about this day," said Stevie. "I'll remember you guys and Tumbleweed and San Antonio Sal . . ."

"And Gabriel," teased Lisa.

"Yes, and Gabriel," Stevie admitted with a smile. "You know, I think you guys were right. He and I do have a mutual crush going. As much as I hated the idea of having to kiss him in front of everybody, I'll have to admit that I do kind of wonder what it might have been like."

"So, what's stopping you?" laughed Carole. "The party's just beginning."

Stevie rubbed the belt buckle. "I don't know. I guess I'm not really, *really* interested in him." She shrugged. "I mean, he's cute and good-looking and he has a lot of nice qualities, but he can't hold a candle to Phil."

"But, Stevie, you've worried that your relationship with Phil was over ever since we started this trip," said Lisa. "You've convinced yourself that he's fallen for another girl."

"I know." Stevie sighed. "I just realized when I saw Gabriel blow me that kiss that he and I have really been flirting with each other the whole time. Oh, I know that competing in contests and calling each other names

109

doesn't seem like flirting, but in this case, that's what it was." She looked at her friends. "And if I can flirt with Gabriel, how can I expect Phil not to flirt with that cute redhead who's on the raft with him? I mean, it wouldn't be fair!"

Carole and Lisa looked at each other and shook their heads. Only Stevie Lake could stew for a whole week about Phil Marsten, grumble about Gabriel Jackson, get herself bamboozled by a goat, save Carole's life, and then decide that she'd had a crush on Gabriel all along and she didn't mind if Phil flirted with a cute redhead who probably didn't even exist!

Carole gave a low whistle. "Stevie," she said, "when you want to, you sure can cover a lot of ground!"

Just then the band played a single loud chord and Mr. Williams turned the microphone back on. "Okay, everybody. Now Dashing Dan and His Prairie Dog Band are going to provide music for square dancing. All the tables up front have been cleared away, so grab a partner and form your squares!"

Jeremy Barksdale came over and asked Lisa to dance, while a cute boy who'd competed in the calf roping contest grabbed Carole's hand. As Stevie watched her friends join the dancers, she felt a tap on her shoulder.

"May I have this dance, ma'am?"

Stevie turned. Gabriel, smiling, was holding his arm out for her. She rose and took it, and together they walked to the dance floor.

"I've got to admit this is the first time I've ever danced with a girl who had a championship rodeo belt buckle," Gabriel said as they joined hands for a large Texas star.

"Well, this is the first time I've ever danced with a boy who could pin a goat in eight seconds," Stevie laughed.

"And tie a calf in ten," he added. "And win the quarter-mile race in—"

"Okay, okay," said Stevie. "It's just a shame that we'll never know who would have really won the rodeo."

Gabriel smiled. "Oh, I don't know," he said as he put his arm snugly around her waist and swung her in a tight circle. "I kind of think we both did."

"Isn't it wonderful to be home?" Lisa sat on a bale of hay outside Pine Hollow Stables. It was late afternoon, and the girls were watching their horses graze in the front paddock. "I mean, we've got hot showers and soft beds and regular clothes and milk that comes out of a refrigerator instead of out of a cow!"

Carole looked up from the stack of photographs in her lap and laughed. "Gosh, Lisa. I thought you were really getting into the pioneer spirit."

"Oh, don't get me wrong. I mean, I really enjoyed the trip and the rodeo and all the people we met," Lisa said. "I guess I just learned a lot about myself, too."

"Like what?" asked Carole.

"Like even though it's neat to do things the way the

pioneers did them, I really like living today a whole lot better."

"I know what you mean," said Carole. "Experiencing the past is great, but it's the modern age we've got to deal with today."

"I wonder if she has brown eyes or green eyes?" Stevie worried out loud as she tapped her foot nervously in the dust.

Carole frowned. "Who?"

"Phil's new girlfriend," Stevie said morosely, cupping her chin in her hand.

"Maybe she's got one of each," suggested Lisa. "There's a girl in my class like that. It's really cool."

"Or maybe she's got one of all three," Carole laughed. "One blue, one green, and one brown, right in the middle of her forehead! That would certainly get Phil's attention."

"Ha, ha, ha," Stevie said while her friends collapsed in giggles beside her. "You two don't seem to be taking this nearly as seriously as I am."

"I'm sorry, Stevie." Lisa wiped tears of laughter from her eyes. "It's just that this wonderful, beautiful, incredibly smart girl is all you've thought about ever since we've been back. Haven't you talked to Phil about her on the phone?"

"No. We've just played phone tag with each other. I leave him a message, and then he leaves me one back."

Stevie checked her watch. "He's supposed to be here in five minutes to go with us to TD's."

"Good," said Carole. "In five minutes we'll probably find out that this mysterious redhead is just a product of your overactive imagination, and we can talk about something else for a change."

"Like what?" asked Stevie.

"Like how much Deborah liked the outline we did for her," said Lisa. "You know, she seemed really surprised. I don't think she thought we would come up with something that good."

"Well, we had a lot of help with it," Carole said. "We had the photos Polly Shaver gave us, and Gabriel helped, too. He told us a bunch of historical stuff that was really neat." Carole held up one of the snapshots. "Look, Lisa. Here's that picture Polly took of you milking Veronica!"

The girls looked at the picture. Veronica the cow stood gazing at the camera while Lisa grinned from the milking stool.

"I'm going to hang that up over Veronica diAngelo's cubby," Lisa laughed as she studied the picture more closely. "I think she needs to know that somewhere out West, walking the Oregon Trail, is a perfectly nice cow that shares her name."

"I wonder what her name is?" Stevie said glumly.

Carole frowned and waved the picture. "Stevie, it's Veronica! Don't you remember?"

"No, not the cow. Phil's new girlfriend. I used to think

114

it was probably Meghan or Chelsea, but now I'm leaning toward Kelli. Or maybe Jennifer."

"*Arrrgggghhhh!*" groaned Carole. "I give up!"

"Look!" Stevie cried. "Here he comes!"

The girls watched as the Marstens' station wagon slowly rolled up the Pine Hollow driveway. Lisa and Carole exchanged smiles.

"I think now would be the perfect time to pin this picture over Veronica's cubby," Carole suggested with a wink.

"I think you're absolutely right." Lisa nodded vigorously. "This scene might be too awful for our tender eyes to see." Quietly they tiptoed back inside the stable.

"Phil!" Stevie cried, running toward him as soon as he was out of the car.

"Hi, Stevie!" he called, hurrying to meet her.

They met halfway between the stable and the driveway and gave each other a big hug.

"It's so good to see you!" said Phil, grinning down at her. His trip had left him with a much deeper tan and a peeling nose, but otherwise he looked the same. His eyes still twinkled and his smile was still warm.

"Oh, me too," Stevie replied with a grin. "Did you have a good vacation?"

"It was terrific," he said. "How about yours?"

"Oh, it was so much fun! We got out there and we were assigned roles to play and we had to wear period costumes, which meant I had to drive a team of horses all day in a dress! Lisa was in charge of this cow named Veronica, and Carole stayed in the saddle from sunup till dusk." The words seemed to tumble out of Stevie's mouth.

"Then there was this bratty little kid named Eileen, and her teddy bear was the only thing we couldn't pull out of the river when her wagon got swamped. Then she cried over it so hard that she started a cattle stampede, and we had to jump on these cowponies bareback and—"

Phil's green eyes grew wide. He laughed. "Stevie! Slow down! You're making your vacation sound like a Wild West movie!"

"Well, it was, in a way." Stevie stopped and took a breath. "We met some really neat people on the trip, too. There was Jeremy Barksdale, the wagon master; Mr. Cate from Alabama; Polly Shaver from Cincinnati; Gabri—" Stevie stopped abruptly. In the excitement of seeing Phil, she'd forgotten all about Gabriel. But suddenly his blue eyes and his dimples popped into her head, right along with the beautiful redhead with whom she'd pictured Phil rafting down the river. *Now is the time*, she thought, summoning her courage as they strolled hand in hand to the stable. *I'm going to find out about Phil's new love.*

"But that's enough about my trip," she said, squeezing his hand and gazing up at him adoringly. "Tell me about yours."

"Well, we met up with our outfitters at Rattlesnake

Junction. We had a flotilla of four rafts, each carrying twelve people. Every raft had a guide in it, because some of the white water was pretty rough. Our raft capsized twice, and my mom lost her favorite pair of sunglasses." Phil shuddered. "And man, when you got washed over-board you really felt it. That water was cold!"

"Who went with you?" Stevie asked innocently.

"Our guide was Hank Parker. He's been rafting for years, and he knew all the best places along the river to stop. He had this really neat fishing rod that folded up small enough to carry in your shirt pocket."

"Really?" Stevie pretended to be impressed with the fishing rod. "Who else went along?"

"Huh?" Phil looked at her and frowned. "Well, let's see. There were some newlyweds from Atlanta and some retired people from Arizona, and there was the Lin family. They'd flown all the way over from Taiwan just to go rafting."

"That's great, but was there anybody really interesting on your raft?" Stevie persisted.

"Sure. We rode with Mr. Feeney, who recited poetry every time we paddled through rapids; and a guy named Chip, who I played Hacky Sack with, and . . ." Phil thought a minute, then broke into a wide grin. "And there was Red."

"Red?" Stevie repeated weakly.

"Yes. Red." Phil's eyes took on a dreamy look. "Man, she is great."

117

"Great?" Stevie's stomach grew queasy. She had been right all along!

"Yeah. She is so cool. And so smart. We played ball for hours. She even likes soccer and she can swim like a fish." Phil gave a little laugh. "And she loves barbecued potato chips!"

"Potato chips?" Stevie frowned, her face now growing red with anger.

"Yeah, she's great. Every night after supper we would fool around for hours. Then, when we were both exhausted, she'd jump into my arms and give me a big kiss!"

Stevie suddenly dropped Phil's hand. She turned to him, her eyes blazing. "You've got a lot of nerve, Phil Marsten! First you come over here pretending to have missed me, then you start telling me about this wonderful redhead who leaps into your arms and kisses you every night!"

Stevie turned on her heel and walked toward the paddock, where Belle was happily browsing through the grass. Horses, she thought, were dependable. Guys were not.

She heard footsteps following her. "Wait, Stevie," she heard Phil call. "It's not what you think!"

He hurried up behind her and tapped her on the shoulder. "Hey," he said with a laugh. "Red's nobody to be upset about. Red's a dog!"

Stevie whirled around to face him. "Phil Marsten, that's an even jerkier thing to say! Now you're going to tell me that even though this girl is wonderful and funny and smart, you really couldn't like her because she's not very pretty! I think you're the shallowest person I've ever met!"

"No, wait, Stevie," Phil protested. He dropped to the ground, held his hands up like paws, and pretended to pant. "Red really *is* a dog!" he cried. "Like *arf, arf!* Like fetch! Like roll over and play dead!"

Stevie looked down at Phil. Though she was still mad at him, it was hard not to laugh at his goofy dog imitation. "Really?" she said, raising one eyebrow.

He leaped to his feet. "Yes. She's Mr. Feeney's Irish setter. I can show you pictures of her. You can ask my mom and dad."

"Really?" Stevie repeated.

He nodded.

"Oh, Phil," she said. She threw her arms around his neck.

"You know, I'm surprised you'd think I would go rafting and fall for somebody else." Phil sounded hurt.

"I'm sorry," she said as she hugged him. "The whole time I was gone it just seemed so real. And the more I thought about it, the more real it became." She looked at him. "And you *were* involved with a redhead, in a way."

"I know." Phil sighed. "It'll be tough waking up every morning without those big brown eyes looking into mine, begging me to throw a stick!"

"Oh, I think you'll get over it," Stevie laughed, hugging him harder. They stayed like that for a long time.

119

A little farther away, Lisa and Carole tiptoed to the front of the stable.

"How's it going?" Lisa asked, not daring to look at Stevie and Phil.

Carole peeked around the stable door. "It's okay," she reported after a long moment. "They're hugging. They're kissing. If the redhead ever existed, they seem to have gotten over her." She turned to Lisa and grinned. "I think it's safe to come out now!"

"Good!" Lisa sighed with relief. "Now we can go to TD's. Now Stevie will stop talking about the redhead. Now life as we know it will return to normal."

"Terrific." Carole laughed. "It really is wonderful to be home!"

PROLOGUE

"Do you think we'll get there in time?" Stevie Lake asked, looking around for some reassuring sign that the airport was near.

"Since that plane almost landed on us, I think it's safe to say that we're close," Carole Hanson said.

"Turn right here," said Callie Forester from the backseat.

"And then left up ahead," Carole advised, picking out directions from the signs that flashed past near the airport entrance. "I think Lisa's plane is leaving from that terminal there."

"Which one?"

"The one we just passed," Callie said.

"Oh," said Stevie. She gripped the steering wheel tightly and looked for a way to turn around without causing a major traffic tie-up.

"This would be easier if we were on horseback," said Carole.

"Everything's easier on horseback," Stevie agreed.

"Or if we had a police escort," said Callie.

"Have you done that?" Stevie asked, trying to maneuver the car across three lanes of traffic.

"I have," said Callie. "It's kind of fun, but dangerous. It makes you think you're almost as important as other people tell you you are."

Stevie rolled her window down and waved wildly at the confused drivers around her. Clearly, her waving confused them more, but it worked. All traffic stopped. She crossed the necessary three lanes and pulled onto the service road.

It took another ten minutes to get back to the right and then ten more to find a parking place. Five minutes into the terminal. And then all that was left was to find Lisa.

"Where do you think she is?" Carole asked.

"I know," said Stevie. "Follow me."

"That's what we've been doing all morning," Callie said dryly. "And look how far it's gotten us."

But she followed anyway.

ALEX LAKE REACHED across the table in the airport cafeteria and took Lisa Atwood's hand.

"It's going to be a long summer," he said.

Lisa nodded. Saying good-bye was one of her least favorite activities. She didn't want Alex to know how hard it was, though. That would just make it tougher on him. The two of them had known each other for four years—as long as Lisa had been best friends with Alex's twin sister, Stevie. But they'd only started dating six months earlier. Lisa could hardly believe that. It seemed as if she'd been in love with him forever.

"But it is just for the summer," she said. The words sounded dumb even as they came out of her mouth. The summer *was* long. She wouldn't come back to Virginia until right before school started.

"I wish your dad didn't live so far away, and I wish the summer weren't so long."

"It'll go fast," said Lisa.

"For you, maybe. You'll be in California, surfing or something. I'll just be here, mowing lawns."

"I've never surfed in my life—"

"Until now," said Alex. It was almost a challenge, and Lisa didn't like it.

"I don't want to fight with you," said Lisa.

"I don't want to fight with you, either," he said, relenting. "I'm sorry. It's just that I want things to be different. Not very different. Just a little different."

"Me too," said Lisa. She squeezed his hand. It was a way to keep from saying anything else, because she was afraid that if she tried to speak she might cry, and she hated it when she cried. It made her face red and puffy, but most of all, it told other people how she was feeling. She'd found it useful to keep her feelings to herself these days. Like Alex, she wanted things to be different, but she wanted them to be very different, not just a little. She sighed. That was slightly better than crying.

"I TOLD YOU SO," said Stevie to Callie and Carole.

Stevie had threaded her way through the airport terminal, straight to the cafeteria near the security checkpoint. And there, sitting next to the door, were her twin brother and her best friend.

"Surprise!" the three girls cried, crowding around the table.

"We just couldn't let you be the only one to say goodbye to Lisa," Carole said, sliding into the booth next to Alex.

"We had to be here, too. You understand that, don't you?" Stevie asked Lisa as she sat down next to her.

"And since I was in the car, they brought me along," said Callie, pulling up a chair from a nearby table.

"You guys!" said Lisa, her face lighting up with joy. "I'm so glad you're here. I was afraid I wasn't going to see you for months and months!"

She *was* glad they were there. It wouldn't have felt right if she'd had to leave without seeing them one more time. "I thought you had other things to do."

"We just told you that so we could surprise you. We did surprise you, didn't we?"

"You surprised me," Lisa said, beaming.

"Me too," Alex said dryly. "I'm surprised, too. I really thought I could go for an afternoon, just *one* afternoon of my life, without seeing my twin sister."

Stevie grinned. "Well, there's always tomorrow," she said. "And that's something to look forward to, right?"

"Right," he said, grinning back.

Since she was closest to the outside, Callie went and got sodas for herself, Stevie, and Carole. When she rejoined the group, they were talking about everything in the world except the fact that Lisa was going to be gone for the summer and how much they were all going to miss one another.

She passed the drinks around and sat quietly at the end of the table. There wasn't much for her to say. She didn't really feel as if she belonged there. She wasn't anybody's best friend. It wasn't as if they minded her being there, but she'd come along because Stevie had offered to drive her to a tack shop after they left the airport. She was simply along for the ride.

". . . And don't forget to say hello to Skye."

"Skye? Skye who?" asked Alex.

"Don't pay any attention to him," Lisa said. "He's just jealous."

"You mean because Skye is a movie star?"

"And say hi to your father and the new baby. It must be exciting that you'll meet your sister."

"Well, of course, you've already met her, but now she's crawling, right? It's a whole different thing."

An announcement over the PA system brought their chatter to a sudden halt.

"It's my flight," Lisa said slowly. "They're starting to board and I've got to get through security and then to Gate . . . whatever."

"Fourteen," Alex said. "It comes after Gate Twelve. There are no thirteens in airports."

"Let's go."

"Here, I'll carry that."

"And I'll get this one . . ."

As Callie watched, Lisa hugged Carole and Stevie. Then she kissed Alex. Then she hugged her friends again. Then she turned to Alex.

"I think it's time for us to go," Carole said tactfully.

"Write or call every day," Stevie said.

"It's a promise," said Lisa. "Thanks for coming to the airport. You, too, Callie."

Callie smiled and gave Lisa a quick hug before all the girls backed off from Lisa and Alex.

Lisa waved. Her friends waved and turned to leave her alone with Alex. They were all going to miss her, but the girls had one another. Alex only had his lawns to mow. He needed the last minutes with Lisa.

"See you at home!" Stevie called over her shoulder, but she didn't think Alex heard. His attention was completely focused on one person.

Carole wiped a tear from her eye once they'd rounded a corner. "I'm going to miss her."

"Me too," said Stevie.

Carole turned to Callie. "It must be hard for you to understand," she said.

"Not really," said Callie. "I can tell you three are really close."

"We are," Carole said. "Best friends for a long time. We're practically inseparable." Even to her the words sounded exclusive and uninviting. If Callie noticed, she didn't say anything.

The three girls walked out of the terminal and found their way to Stevie's car. As she turned on the engine, Stevie was aware of an uncomfortable empty feeling. She really didn't like the idea of Lisa's being gone for the summer, and her own unhappiness was not going to be helped by a brother who was going to spend the entire time moping about his missing girlfriend. There had to be something that would make her feel better.

"Say, Carole, do you want to come along with us to the tack shop?" she asked.

"No, I can't," Carole said. "I promised I'd bring in the horses from the paddock before dark, so you can just drop me off at Pine Hollow. Anyway, aren't you due at work in an hour?"

Stevie glanced at her watch. Carole was right. Everything was taking longer than it was supposed to this afternoon.

"Don't worry," Callie said quickly. "We can go to the tack shop another time."

"You don't mind?" Stevie asked.

"No. I don't. Really," said Callie. "I don't want you to be late for work—either of you. If my parents decide to get a pizza for dinner again, I'm going to want it to arrive on time!"

Stevie laughed, but not because she thought anything was very funny. She wasn't about to forget the last time she'd delivered a pizza to Callie's family. In fact, she wished it hadn't happened, but it had. Now she had to find a way to face up to it.

As she pulled out of the airport parking lot, a plane roared overhead, rising into the brooding sky. *Maybe that's Lisa's plane*, she thought. The noise of its flight seemed to mark the beginning of a long summer.

The first splats of rain hit the windshield as Stevie paid their way out of the parking lot. By the time they were on the highway, it was raining hard. The sky had darkened to a steely gray. Streaks of lightning brightened it, only to be followed by thunder that made the girls jump.

The storm had come out of nowhere. Stevie flicked on the windshield wipers and hoped it would go right back to nowhere.

The sky turned almost black as the storm strengthened.

Curtains of rain ripped across the windshield, pounding on the hood and roof of the car. The wipers flicked uselessly at the torrent.

"I hope Fez is okay," said Callie. "He hates thunder, you know."

"I'm not surprised," said Carole, trying to control her voice. It seemed to her that there were a lot of things Fez hated. He was as temperamental as any horse she had ever ridden.

Fez was one of the horses in the paddock. Carole didn't want to upset Callie by telling her that. If she told Callie he'd been turned out, Callie would wonder why he hadn't just been exercised. If she told Callie she'd exercised him, Callie might wonder if he was being overworked. Carole shook her head. What was it about this girl that made Carole so certain that whatever she said, it would be wrong? Why couldn't she say the one thing she really needed to say?

Still, Carole worked at Pine Hollow, and that meant taking care of the horses that were boarding there—and that meant keeping the owners happy.

"I'm sure Fez will be fine. Ben and Max will look after him," Carole said.

"I guess you're right," said Callie. "I know he can be difficult. Of course, you've ridden him, so you know that, too. I mean, that's obvious. But it's spirit, you see. Spirit is the key to an endurance specialist. He's got it, and I think he's got the makings of a champion. We'll work together this summer, and come fall . . . well, you'll see."

Spirit—yes, it was important in a horse. Carole knew

that. She just wished she understood why it was that Fez's spirit was so irritating to her. She'd always thought of herself as someone who'd never met a horse she didn't like. Maybe it was the horse's owner . . .

"Uh-oh," said Stevie, putting her foot gently on the brake. "I think I got it going a little too fast there."

"You've got to watch out for that," Callie said. "My father says the police practically lie in wait for teenage drivers. They love to give us tickets. Well, they certainly had fun with me."

"You got a ticket?" Stevie asked.

"No, I just got a warning, but it was almost worse than a ticket. I was going four miles over the speed limit in our hometown. The policeman stopped me, and when he saw who I was, he just gave me a warning. Dad was furious—at me and at the officer, though he didn't say anything to the officer. He was angry at him because he thought someone would find out and say I'd gotten special treatment! I was only going four miles over the speed limit. Really. Even the officer said that. Well, it would have been easier if I'd gotten a ticket. Instead, I got grounded. Dad won't let me drive for three months. Of course, that's nothing compared to what happened to Scott last year."

"What happened to Scott?" Carole asked, suddenly curious about the driving challenges of the Forester children.

"Well, it's kind of a long story," said Callie. "But—"

"Wow! Look at that!" Stevie interrupted. There was an amazing streak of lightning over the road ahead. The dark afternoon brightened for a minute. Thunder followed instantly.

"Maybe we should pull off the road or something?" Carole suggested.

"I don't think so," said Stevie. She squinted through the windshield. "It's not going to last long. It never does when it rains this hard. We get off at the next exit anyway."

She slowed down some more and turned the wipers up a notch. She followed the car in front of her, keeping a constant eye on the two red spots of the car's taillights. She'd be okay as long as she could see them. The rain pelted the car so loudly that it was hard to talk. Stevie drove on cautiously.

Then, as suddenly as it had started, the rain stopped. Stevie spotted the sign for their exit, signaled, and pulled off to the right and up the ramp. She took a left onto the overpass and followed the road toward Willow Creek.

The sky was as dark as it had been, and there were clues that there had been some rain there, but nothing nearly as hard as the rain they'd left on the interstate. Stevie sighed with relief and switched the windshield wipers to a slower rate.

"I think I'll drop you off at Pine Hollow first," she said, turning onto the road that bordered the stable's property.

Pine Hollow's white fences followed the contour of the road, breaking the open, grassy hillside into a sequence of paddocks and fields. A few horses stood in the fields, swishing their tails. One bucked playfully and ran up a hill, shaking his head to free his mane in the wind. Stevie smiled. Horses always seemed to her the most welcoming sight in the world.

"Then I'll take Callie home," Stevie continued, "and

after that I'll go over to Pizza Manor. I may be a few minutes late for work, but who orders pizza at five o'clock in the afternoon anyway?"

"Now, now," teased Carole. "Is that any way for you to mind your Pizza Manors?"

"Well, at least I have my hat with me," said Stevie. Or did she? She looked into the rearview mirror to see if she could spot it, and when that didn't do any good, she glanced over her shoulder. Callie picked it up and started to hand it to her.

"Here," she said. "We wouldn't want— Wow! I guess the storm isn't over yet!"

The sky had suddenly filled with a brilliant streak of lightning, jagged and pulsating, accompanied by an explosion of thunder.

It startled Stevie. She shrieked and turned her face back to the road. The light was so sudden and so bright that it blinded her for a second. The car swerved. Stevie braked. She clutched at the steering wheel and then realized she couldn't see because the rain was pelting even harder than before. She reached for the wiper control, switching it to its fastest speed.

There was something to her right! She saw something move, but she didn't know what it was.

"Stevie!" Carole cried.

"Look out!" Callie screamed from the backseat.

Stevie swerved to the left on the narrow road, hoping it would be enough. Her answer was a sickening jolt as the car slammed into something solid. The car spun around, smashing against the thing again. When the thing screamed, Stevie knew it was a horse. Then it disappeared from her field of vision. Once again, the car spun. It smashed against the guardrail on the left side of the road and tumbled up and over it as if the rail had never been there.

Down they went, rolling, spinning. Stevie could hear the screams of her friends. She could hear her own voice, echoing in the close confines of the car, answered by the thumps of the car rolling down the hillside into a gully. Suddenly the thumping stopped. The screams were stilled. The engine cut off. The wheels stopped spinning. And all Stevie could hear was the idle *slap*, *slap*, *slap* of her windshield wipers.

"Carole?" she whispered. "Are you okay?"

"I think so. What about you?" Carole answered.

"Me too. Callie? Are you okay?" Stevie asked.

There was no answer.

"Callie?" Carole echoed.

The only response was the girl's shallow breathing. How could this have happened?

ABOUT THE AUTHOR

BONNIE BRYANT is the author of more than a hundred books about horses, including The Saddle Club series, The Saddle Club Super Editions, the Pony Tails series, and Pine Hollow, which follows the Saddle Club girls into their teens. She has also written novels and movie novelizations under her married name, B. B. Hiller.

Ms. Bryant began writing The Saddle Club in 1986. Although she had done some riding before that, she intensified her studies then and found herself learning right along with her characters Stevie, Carole, and Lisa. She claims that they are all much better riders than she is.

Ms. Bryant was born and raised in New York City. She still lives there, in Greenwich Village, with her two sons.